Great English Monarchs

and their Times

英國名君偉績

商務印書館

This Chinese edition of *Great English Monarchs and their Times* has been published with the written permission of Black Cat Publishing.

The copyright of this Chinese edition is owned by The Commercial Press (H.K.) Ltd.

Name of Book: Great English Monarchs and their Times
Author: Gina D. B. Clemen
Editor: Claudia Fiocco
Design: Nadia Maestri
Edition: ©2000 Black Cat Publishing
              an imprint of Cideb Editrice, Genoa, Canterbury

系　列　名：Black Cat 優質英語階梯閱讀 · Level 3
書　　　名：英國名君偉績
顧　　　問：Angeli Lau
責任編輯：金　堅
封面設計：張　毅
出　　　版：商務印書館 (香港) 有限公司
　　　　　香港筲箕灣耀興道3號東滙廣場8樓
　　　　　http://www.commercialpress.com.hk
印　　　刷：中華商務彩色印刷有限公司
　　　　　香港新界大埔汀麗路36號中華商務印刷大廈
版　　　次：2003年12月第1版第2次印刷
　　　　　© 2003 商務印書館 (香港) 有限公司
　　　　　ISBN 962 07 1643 4
　　　　　Printed in Hong Kong

出版説明

　　本館一向倡導優質閱讀，近年來連續推出了以 "Q" 為標識的 "Quality English Learning 優質英語學習" 系列，其中《讀名著學英語》叢書，更是香港書展入選好書，讀者反響令人鼓舞。推動社會閱讀風氣，推動英語經典閱讀，藉閱讀拓廣世界視野，提高英語水平，已經成為一種潮流。

　　然良好閱讀習慣的養成非一日之功，大多數初、中級程度的讀者，常視直接閱讀厚重的原著為畏途。如何給年輕的讀者提供切實的指引和幫助，如何既提供優質的學習素材，又提供名師的教學方法，是當下社會關注的重要問題。 針對這種情況，本館特別延請香港名校名師，根據多年豐富的教學經驗，精選海外適合初、中級英語程度讀者的優質經典讀物，有系統地出版了這套叢書，名為《Black Cat 優質英語階梯閱讀》。

　　《Black Cat 優質英語階梯閱讀》體現了香港名校名師堅持經典學習的教學理念，以及多年行之有效的學習方法。既有經過改寫和縮寫的經典名著，又有富創意的現代作品；既有精心設計的聽、説、讀、寫綜合練習，又有豐富的歷史文化知識；既有彩色插圖、繪圖和照片，又有英美專業演員朗讀作品的 CD。適合口味不同的讀者享受閱讀之樂，欣賞經典之美。

　　《Black Cat 優質英語階梯閱讀》由淺入深，逐階提升，好像參與一個尋寶遊戲，入門並不難，但要真正尋得寶藏，需要投入，更需要堅持。只有置身其中的人，才能體味純正英語的魅力，領略得到真寶的快樂。當英語閱讀成為自己生活的一部分，英語水平的提高自然水到渠成。

商務印書館 (香港) 有限公司
編輯部

使用説明

 應該怎樣選書?

按閱讀興趣選書

《Black Cat 優質英語階梯閱讀》精選世界經典作品,也包括富於創意的現代作品;既有膾炙人口的小説、戲劇,又有非小説類的文化知識讀物,品種豐富,內容多樣,適合口味不同的讀者挑選自己感興趣的書,享受閱讀的樂趣。

按英語程度選書

《Black Cat 優質英語階梯閱讀》現設 Level 1 至 Level 6,由淺入深,涵蓋初、中級英語程度。讀物分級採用了國際上通用的劃分標準,主要以詞彙 (vocabulary) 和結構 (structures) 劃分。

Level 1 至 Level 3 出現的詞彙較淺顯,相對深的核心詞彙均配上中文解釋,節省讀者查找詞典的時間,以專心理解正文內容。在註釋的幫助下,讀者若能流暢地閱讀正文內容,就不用擔心這一本書程度過深。

Level 1 至 Level 3 出現的動詞時態形式和句子結構比較簡單。動詞時態形式以現在時 (present simple)、現在時進行式 (present continuous)、過去時 (past simple) 為主,句子結構大部分是簡單句 (simple sentences)。此外,還包括比較級和最高級 (comparative and superlative forms)、可數和不可數名詞 (countable and uncountable nouns) 以及冠詞 (articles) 等語法知識點。

Level 4 至 Level 6 出現的動詞時態形式,以現在完成時 (present perfect)、現在完成時進行式 (present perfect continuous)、過去完成時 (past perfect continuous) 為主,句子結構大部分是複合句 (compound sentences)、條件從句 (1st and 2nd conditional sentences) 等。此外,還包括情態動詞 (modal verbs)、被動形式 (passive forms)、動名詞

（gerunds）、短語動詞（phrasal verbs）等語法知識點。

根據上述的語法範圍，讀者可按自己實際的英語水平，如詞彙量、語法知識、理解能力、閱讀能力等自主選擇，不再受制於學校年級劃分或學歷高低的約束，完全根據個人需要選擇合適的讀物。

② 怎樣提高閱讀效果？

閱讀的方法主要有兩種：一是泛讀，二是精讀。兩者各有功能，適當地結合使用，相輔相成，有事半功倍之效。

泛讀，指閱讀大量適合自己程度（可稍淺，但不能過深）、不同內容、風格、體裁的讀物，但求明白內容大意，不用花費太多時間鑽研細節，主要作用是多接觸英語，減輕對它的生疏感，鞏固以前所學過的英語，讓腦子在潛意識中吸收詞彙用法、語法結構等。

精讀，指小心認真地閱讀內容精彩、組織有條理、遣詞造句又正確的作品，着重點在於理解"準確"及"深入"，欣賞其精彩獨到之處。精讀時，可充分利用書中精心設計的練習，學習掌握有用的英語詞彙和語法知識。精讀後，可再花十分鐘朗讀其中一小段有趣的文字，邊唸邊細心領會文字的結構和意思。

《Black Cat 優質英語階梯閱讀》中的作品均值得精讀，如時間有限，不妨嘗試每兩個星期泛讀一本，輔以每星期挑選書中一章精彩的文字精讀。要學好英語，持之以恆地泛讀和精讀英文是最有效的方法。

③ 本系列的練習與測試有何功能？

《Black Cat 優質英語階梯閱讀》特別注重練習的設計，為讀者考慮周到，切合實用需求，學習功能強。每章後均配有訓練聽、說、讀、寫四項技能的練習，分量、難度恰到好處。

聽力練習分兩類，一是重聽故事回答問題，二是聆聽主角對話、書信朗讀、或模擬記者訪問後寫出答案，旨在以生活化的練習形式逐步提高聽力。每本書均配有 CD 提供作品朗讀，朗讀者都是專業演員，英國作品由英國演員錄音，美國作品由美國演員錄音，務求增加聆聽的真實感和感染力。多聆聽英式和美式英語兩種發音，可讓讀者熟悉二者的差異，逐漸培養分辨英美發音的能力，提高聆聽理解的準確度。此外，模仿錄音朗讀故事或模仿主人翁在戲劇中的對白，都是訓練口語能力的好方法。

閱讀理解練習形式多樣化，有縱橫字謎、配對、填空、字句重組等等，注重訓練讀者的理解、推敲和聯想等多種閱讀技能。

寫作練習尤具新意，教讀者使用網式圖示（spidergrams）記錄重點，採用問答、書信、電報、記者採訪等多樣化形式，鼓勵讀者動手寫作。

書後更設有升級測試（Exit Test）及答案，供讀者檢查學習效果。充分利用書中的練習和測試，可全面提升聽、說、讀、寫四項技能。

❹ 本系列還能提供甚麼幫助？

《Black Cat 優質英語階梯閱讀》提倡豐富多元的現代閱讀，巧用書中提供的資訊，有助於提升英語理解力，擴闊視野。

每本書都設有專章介紹相關的歷史文化知識，經典名著更有作者生平、社會背景等資訊。書內富有表現力的彩色插圖、繪圖和照片，使閱讀充滿趣味，部分加上如何解讀古典名畫的指導，增長見識。有的書還提供一些與主題相關的網址，比如關於不同國家的節慶源流的網址，讓讀者多利用網上資源增進知識。

Contents

PART ONE   **HENRY VIII – A TUDOR KING**   9
亨利八世 — 都鐸君王

Introduction   10

CHAPTER ONE   The Young King 少年國王   11

UNDERSTANDING THE TEXT   15

CHAPTER TWO   War, Peace and Taxes   19
戰爭、和平與徵稅

UNDERSTANDING THE TEXT   25

'Reading' a Painting 解讀油畫   27

CHAPTER THREE   The Break with Rome   30
與羅馬教廷決裂

UNDERSTANDING THE TEXT   35

CHAPTER FOUR   Henry's Later Years   38
亨利的晚年

UNDERSTANDING THE TEXT   43

PART TWO   **ELIZABETH I – THE VIRGIN QUEEN**   47
伊利莎伯一世 — 不結婚的女王

Introduction   48

CHAPTER ONE   Young Elizabeth   49
年輕的伊利莎伯

UNDERSTANDING THE TEXT   53

CHAPTER TWO   Plots and Problems   56
宮廷謀反與困擾

UNDERSTANDING THE TEXT   60

CHAPTER THREE   Exploration and Discovery   64
探索與發現

UNDERSTANDING THE TEXT   69

	CHAPTER FOUR	The Spanish Armada	72
		西班牙無敵艦隊	
		UNDERSTANDING THE TEXT	79
		'Reading' a Painting 解讀油畫	81

PART THREE		**VICTORIA – MOTHER OF THE EMPIRE**	85
		維多利亞—帝國之母	
		Introduction	86
	CHAPTER ONE	The Lonely Princess	87
		孤獨的公主	
		UNDERSTANDING THE TEXT	91
	CHAPTER TWO	The Growth of Commerce and Industry 工商業大興	94
		UNDERSTANDING THE TEXT	100
	CHAPTER THREE	Wars and Loss	103
		戰爭與喪夫	
		UNDERSTANDING THE TEXT	107
	CHAPTER FOUR	The End of an Era	109
		大時代的結束	
		UNDERSTANDING THE TEXT	115
APPENDICES		**Exit Test**	117
		升級測試	
		Key to the Exercises and Exit Test	123
		練習答案和測試答案	

PET Cambridge Preliminary English Test-style exercises

The story is recorded in full. 故事錄音

This symbol indicates the exercises featured on the accompanying CD. 聽力練習的錄音標記

PART ONE

Portrait of Henry VIII, by Hans the Younger Holbein (1497-8 – 1543).
Belvoir Castle/Bridgeman Art Library.

HENRY VIII – A TUDOR KING

INTRODUCTION

To understand the English monarchs it is important to understand
their times. Today some of their actions seem cruel or extravagant. [1]
But remember that their times were very different from ours.
A king or queen of the 16th century had unlimited power.
Everyone wanted to please the monarch. Rebels [2] or enemies were
eliminated! Executions were a common event in Europe.

Henry VIII was the son of Henry VII, the first Tudor King.
He became king during the Renaissance, [3] a time of great change.
The Renaissance brought new ideas to art, science and philosophy.
However, many of these new ideas clashed [4] with the church. So, the
church and religion changed with the Reformation. [5] The geography
of the world changed too. Explorers discovered new lands, new
people and new products.

All his life Henry VIII desperately wanted a male heir [6] to keep the
Tudors on the throne of England.
He had a very complex personality. [7] He had his faults but he was a
brilliant, talented man and an unforgettable monarch.

---

1. **extravagant**：揮霍無度的。
2. **rebels**：叛亂分子。
3. **Renaissance**：歐洲文藝復興（見頁**17**）。
4. **clashed**：有重大分歧。
5. **Reformation**：宗教改革。
6. **male heir**：男繼承人。
7. **complex personality**：複雜性格。

The Young King

enry VIII became king in 1509, just before his eighteenth birthday. Young Henry was not prepared to be king. He became king only because his elder brother, Arthur, died at the age of fifteen.

Soon after the coronation [1] Henry married his first wife, Catherine of Aragon, who was his brother Arthur's widow. [2]

Catherine was the only child of King Ferdinand of Spain. Spain was then a very powerful country. This marriage created a strong alliance [3] between the two countries.

Catherine was beautiful and intelligent, and Henry loved her. For almost twenty years they were the perfect royal couple and were happy together.

The new King looked like a hero. Henry was handsome and robust. [4] He was six foot (1.83 metres) tall. At that time most men

---

1. **coronation** : 加冕。
2. **widow** : 寡婦。
3. **alliance** : 聯盟。
4. **robust** : 壯健的。

were about five foot four inches (1.60 metres) tall. He had bright blue eyes and red hair. He also had a strong personality. The people of England liked King Henry.

Young Henry was strong and full of energy. He loved playing tennis, riding horses and hunting. He hunted in the forests with hawks. [1] He was a very skilled swordsman and loved mock [2] fights called jousts.

Henry was also a great scholar. He spoke English, French, Latin and Spanish. He studied ancient Greek, religious writings, mathematics and astronomy. He was an avid [3] reader and encouraged others to read too. He loved music and played several instruments very well: the harp, the organ, the lute [4] and

Henry VIII jousts before Catherine of Aragon (1511).

1. **hawks** :
2. **mock** : 模擬。

3. **avid** : 非常熱衷的。
4. **lute** : 詩琴。

Catherine of Aragon, by Michael Sittow.
Kunsthistorisches Museum, Vienna.

the virginals. [1] He was a good singer and dancer, and also composed beautiful songs. We can still listen to some of his compositions.

During this time the Renaissance developed in England. King Henry was a patron [2] of the arts. Writers, poets, painters and musicians were all welcome at his court. The famous Dutch scholar, Erasmus, was Henry's friend.

The young King was very busy with banquets, dancing, hunting and sports. He decorated his castles and palaces with beautiful furniture and paintings. He wore expensive clothes and jewellery, and was generous with his friends.

Henry did not have much time to govern his country. One of his advisers [3] began to govern England. His name was Thomas Wolsey, a clever man of humble origins. [4] He was a cardinal [5] of the Church.

Henry desperately [6] wanted an heir to the Tudor throne. Early in 1511 Catherine gave birth to a son. There were great celebrations, but the little Prince died after two months. King Henry was very disappointed.

---

1. **virginals**：16-17世紀鍵盤樂器。
2. **patron**：贊助人。
3. **advisers**：參謀。
4. **of humble origins**：出身寒微。
5. **cardinal**：樞機主教。
6. **desperately**：極之。

UNDERSTANDING THE TEXT

 Choose the correct answer.

a. Henry VIII became king in 1509
- [ ] just after his fifteenth birthday
- [ ] just before his eighteenth birthday
- [ ] when his sister died

b. Henry's first wife, Catherine of Aragon, was
- [ ] King Ferdinand's youngest sister
- [ ] his brother's best friend
- [ ] his brother's widow and King Ferdinand's only child

c. Young Henry was robust and handsome,
- [ ] but he did not like sports or hunting
- [ ] but he was not tall
- [ ] and he loved hunting and sports

d. He was a great scholar, an avid reader and
- [ ] an excellent musician
- [ ] a good painter
- [ ] a courageous explorer

e. During Henry's reign
- [ ] there were wars between England and Spain
- [ ] the Medieval Ages began
- [ ] the Renaissance developed in England

f. Thomas Wolsey began to govern the country
- [ ] when Henry's brother died
- [ ] because young Henry was busy with banquets, hunting and sports
- [ ] because young Henry became very ill

g. King Henry was very unhappy when
- [ ] his two-month old son died
- [ ] Cardinal Wolsey began to govern the country
- [ ] Catherine of Aragon died

The Past Simple

Go back to Chapter One and underline in pencil the Past Simple of the following verbs. Then write the Past Simple and the Past Participle of each verb in the correct column.

Infinitive （不定式）	Past Simple （簡單過去時）	Past Participle （過去分詞）
to become		
to be		
to die		
to marry		
to love		
to look		
to have		
to speak		
to study		
to play		
to develop		
to begin		

Now circle the regular verbs（規則動詞）**in the first column in green and the irregular verbs in red.**

Think about this

Renaissance is a French word that means rebirth, to be born again. The Renaissance took place in Europe between the 14th and 16th centuries. During this time the art, literature and ideas of ancient Greece were discovered again and studied. This caused many changes in the way of thinking.

Consult an encyclopedia to find answers for the following questions.

a. When did the Renaissance develop?

b. In which cities or regions can you see Renaissance art today?

c. Write the names of two famous people of the Renaissance.

d. What did they do?

 Look at the picture, 'Henry VIII jousts before Catherine of Aragon' (1511) on page 12.
At the joust Henry is dressed like a knight. He is celebrating the birth of his son. Catherine of Aragon watches on the stand with ladies of the court.

1. The painter helps us identify the King by using a symbol. Can you see it? Where is it?

2. Which is the King's horse?
a. the brown one
b. the grey one

3. Which weapons are used by the knights in the joust?
a. swords
b. lances
c. bows

4. The lances are
a. broken
b. intact
c. on the ground

5. The men on the left are
   a. cheering
   b. crying
   c. sad

6. Which moment of the joust is represented? The knights have
   a. already fought
   b. are fighting now
   c. will fight soon

7. Jousts were
   a. real fights where knights killed each other
   b. ceremonial representations of fighting where nobody
   was killed, except accidentally

8. Are there historic jousts in your country today? If so, do
   you think they
   a. reflect your society?
   b. give young men the possibility to use weapons?
   c. are shows which celebrate the past and entertain
   tourists?

9. Jousts are often presented in films at the cinema. Do you
   remember seeing any joust scene? Which film was it? When
   and where did the story take place?

 Listen to the music again.
It was written by Henry VIII.

   a. When you listen to this music, can you imagine people
   dancing at Henry's court?
   b. Do you recognise any of the musical instruments?
   c. Does it sound like any rock group you know?
   d. Could you dance to this type of music?
   e. Can you play a musical instrument?

CHAPTER TWO

War, Peace and Taxes

King Henry was a very ambitious [1] man. He wanted the glory of a war and in 1512 he invaded [2] France unsuccessfully.

The following year Henry was more successful. The English won a battle that Henry called 'The Battle of the Spurs'.

While Henry was in France, the Scottish King, James IV, invaded northern England. After a violent battle the English won at Flodden Field. King James IV and thousands of Scots were killed.

Henry was pleased with the success in France and he wanted to return the following year. However, the war cost a lot of money and only a little land was conquered.

Henry's adviser, Cardinal Thomas Wolsey, did not want another war. He convinced Henry to make peace with France.

---

1. **ambitious** : 野心大的。

2. **invaded** : 侵略。

He was a very ambitious and greedy man. [1] In 1515 he became Lord Chancellor [2] of England. He was the most powerful man in the country after the King! Wolsey became very rich. He used his money to build the 1,000-room palace of Hampton Court. He later gave it to Henry to win his favour.

During this period there were many religious problems. The Catholic Church was very powerful and very rich. Many people in England did not like the Church or the priests. They were tired of paying high taxes to the Church.

In October 1517 a German monk [3] called Martin Luther protested against the Catholic Church. He wanted to make radical [4] changes. This was the beginning of the Reformation and the Protestant Church.

Henry did not like Martin Luther's ideas and wrote the 'Defence of the Seven Sacraments.' He dedicated [5] it to Pope Leo X. The Pope was pleased and gave Henry the title of 'Defender of the Faith.'

For eight years Cardinal Wolsey kept peace with France. In 1520 he organised a meeting in Piccardy in France, between the two Kings. Wolsey wanted the Kings to sign a peace treaty.

Elaborate [6] tents made of gold cloth and a beautiful palace were created for the two Kings and their courts. The entire English court of 5,800 people went to Piccardy. There were jousts and

---

1. **greedy man**：貪婪的人。
2. **Lord Chancellor**：當時的英國宰相。
3. **monk**：
4. **radical**：徹底的。
5. **dedicated**：奉獻給。
6. **elaborate**：精美的。

Thomas Wolsey, by unknown artist.
By courtesy of The National Portrait Gallery, London.

elaborate banquets. An immense amount of money was spent for this occasion. Henry wore a cloak [1] made of gold cloth. The extravagant finery [2] gave the meeting its name 'The Field of the

1. **cloak** : 長袍。   2. **finery** : 華麗服飾。

Cloth of Gold.' The two Kings signed a peace treaty but after two years they were at war again!

Henry and his court lived in luxury. His clothes and jewels

The Field of the Cloth of Gold, by unknown artist.
The Royal Collection © 1999, Her Majesty Queen Elizabeth II.

were always more magnificent. [1] Henry soon spent most of his father's money.

During almost 20 years of marriage Catherine gave birth to four sons, but they all died. Only a girl, Princess Mary, survived. [2] Henry was desperate. He didn't want a daughter. He wanted a son to become king after his death. Catherine was too old to have other children and Henry lost interest in her.

---

1. **magnificent**：令人嘆為觀止的。
2. **survived**：繼續生存。

UNDERSTANDING THE TEXT

 Fill in the gaps with the words in the castle.

> taxes   luxury   Catholic Church
> peace   Catherine
> meeting   Lord Chancellor
> ambitious   Piccardy
> money   son   Reformation
> killed   France (x2)
> religious   English

a. In 1513 Henry went to war against ....

b. King James IV and thousands of Scots were .... at Flodden Field after a battle with the ....

c. Cardinal Wolsey was very .... and became .... of England in 1515.

d. During this period there were .... problems because many people were tired of paying high .... to the Church.

e. The .... began with Martin Luther's protest against the ....

f. Henry and his court went to .... to sign a .... treaty with the King of .... The .... was called 'The Field of the Cloth of Gold.'

g. Henry soon spent most of his father's .... because he and his court lived in ....

h. .... did not give Henry a .... so he lost interest in her.

You are King Henry VIII and you are at the meeting of the 'Field of the Cloth of Gold'. You want to write a letter to your friend, the great scholar Erasmus, in Rotterdam, telling him about the great event.
Put the verbs in the Past Simple tense and add the articles (冠詞) **and conjunctions** (連詞) **if necessary.**

Dear Erasmus,

Lord Chancellor Wolsey / organise / important meeting /
Piccardy / between me / King of France.
My court / I / leave England / Wednesday.
We / have / good sea voyage.
When / we arrive / it / be / sunny day.
I / wear / my precious cloak.
Everyone / be / amazed.
I / bring / a lot of / splendid clothes / jewels.
On Friday / I / go hunting / in / forest.
On Saturday / there be / a joust.
I / win / of course!
It / be / great fun.
On Sunday / the King / invite / me / my court / to /
magnificent banquet.
We / eat / for seven hours!
Then / we / go / to sleep.

Your friend,
Henry

'Reading' a Painting

In the past artists often painted or sculpted[1] portraits of important people. Before photography was invented, there was no other way to represent them. These portraits showed how people were and how they lived. Portraits were not always true representations of the person. Some people wanted to appear young or good-looking when in reality they were not. When a painting is a true representation of the person, we say the portrait is 'realistic'. When the painting looks better than the person, we say that the portrait is 'idealised'.

Look at the portrait of Henry VIII on page 29.

Look at his clothes. They are made of velvet, silk and fur. There is a lot of gold on his cloak and he is wearing rings on both hands. During Henry's time men wore gold rings with precious stones.

Clothes were very expensive in Henry's time and it often took many years to make them. Several people worked on one piece of clothing. The best clothes could cost as much as whole ships. The children of the nobility[2] wore elaborate clothes like adults. The poor wore very simple clothes.

Look at his legs. He has a ribbon called a garter on his left leg. It has the motto of the Order of the Garter, the highest order of Knighthood, written in ancient French.

Look at how big Henry's body is. When he was older, he became so fat that he was transported to his many palaces in a special vehicle on wheels because he could not walk.

Henry is standing on a splendid Persian carpet. Notice the elaborate tapestry[3] behind him.

---

1. **sculpted** : 雕塑成。　　2. **nobility** : 貴族。　　3. **tapestry** : 掛毯。

Look at the painting and answer the questions.

1. What are the dominant[1] colours of this painting?

2. The structure of this portrait is very simple, because there is nothing in the background except the tapestry. In your opinion, this is because:
   a. the King did not own any decorative object or piece of furniture
   b. the painter was not able to represent the King's furniture
   c. the painter wanted to concentrate all the attention on the King

3. Which words describe Henry's face?
   a. beautiful **c.** large
   b. regal[2] **d.** severe[3]

4. In your opinion which words describe Henry's body?
   a. muscular **c.** broad-shouldered
   b. fat **d.** slim

5. Which words best describe King Henry (his clothes, jewellery, face and body)?
   a. happy **c.** powerful
   b. arrogant[4] **d.** surprised

6. Tapestries, like the one in the portrait, existed in all the King's rooms. Why were they used?
   a. to make the rooms dark
   b. to show how rich the King was
   c. to make the rooms warmer

7. What about your house? The walls are
   a. painted
   b. wall-papered
   c. covered with posters
   d. covered with silk tapestries

---

1. **dominant**：主要的。
2. **regal**：有王者風範的。
3. **severe**：嚴厲的。
4. **arrogant**：傲慢的。

© Belvoir Castle/Bridgeman Art Library.

CHAPTER THREE

The Break with Rome

Early in 1526 Henry met a young English lady of the court. Her name was Anne Boleyn. She had long, black hair and dark eyes. She spoke French and wore elegant [1] French clothes. She was very lively, intelligent and interested in politics. [2] Henry fell in love with her immediately. Several men of the court fell in love with her too. Anne had a sixth finger on her left hand. Her enemies called her a witch! [3]

Henry wanted to marry Anne Boleyn and have a son with her. He decided to divorce Catherine, but he needed permission from the Pope in Rome. He asked Cardinal Wolsey to convince the Pope. After a few years the Pope refused the divorce.

Henry was furious with Wolsey and the Church. He accused Cardinal Wolsey of treason [4] and he died soon after. In 1529 Henry

---

1. **elegant** : 優雅的。

2. **politics** : 政治。

3. **witch** :

4. **treason** : 叛國。

Anne Boleyn, by unknown artist.
By courtesy of The National Portrait Gallery, London.

chose Sir Thomas More, a great scholar and an honest man, as Lord Chancellor of England. Sir Thomas More was Lord Chancellor until 1532 when he was beheaded[1] because he opposed Henry's break with Rome.

In 1533 Henry also chose a new Archbishop of Canterbury, Thomas Cranmer. Cranmer wanted to change the Church. He believed in the absolute power[2] of the King. Cranmer encouraged the use of the Bible in English. He also helped to establish the Protestant Church in England. He later annulled[3] Henry's marriage to Catherine of Aragon.

In January 1533 Henry and Anne Boleyn were secretly married. Catherine of Aragon was banished[4] from court and died alone three years later.

By May 1533 Anne Boleyn was Queen of England. Four months later she gave birth to Princess Elizabeth. Another girl! Henry was desolate.[5] He wanted a son more than anything.

In 1534 Thomas Cromwell, Henry's new Lord Chancellor, helped put into effect the Act of Supremacy. With this Act Henry became the Supreme[6] Head of the Church of England.

Henry was soon tired of Anne because she did not give him a son. He then met another lady called Jane Seymour and fell in love with her.

Anne, Henry's second wife, was accused of adultery and treason. She was imprisoned in the Tower of London and was beheaded in May 1536.

---

1. **beheaded**：斬首。
2. **absolute power**：極權。
3. **annulled**：廢止。
4. **banished**：放逐。
5. **desolate**：悽涼的。
6. **supreme**：至高無上的。

Jane Seymour, by Hans the Younger Holbein (1497-8 – 1543).
Kunsthistorisches Museum, Vienna.

Eleven days after Anne Boleyn's execution Henry married Jane Seymour. She was a quiet, docile [1] lady who brought happiness to the royal family.

In October 1537 Jane gave birth to a son, Prince Edward. King Henry was overjoyed [2] and the whole country celebrated. Unfortunately, after twelve days the Queen died from an infection.

Henry mourned [3] her for a long time. Jane, his third wife, was probably his favourite.

Henry now had an heir – Prince Edward was the future King of England. He was first in succession [4] to the throne because he was a male. Edward was intelligent and received an excellent education from the best scholars.

To show his power and importance Henry VIII built magnificent palaces such as St James' Palace and Whitehall Palace. He also built castles and more than fifty houses around England.

---

1. **docile** : 溫順的。
2. **overjoyed** : 十分高興。
3. **mourned** : 哀悼。
4. **succession** : 繼承。

UNDERSTANDING THE TEXT

1 **Are the following sentences true (T) or false (F)? Correct the false ones.**

	T	F
a. In 1526 Henry fell in love with Anne Boleyn and decided to divorce from his wife. But he needed permission from Cardinal Wolsey.	☐	☐
b. Henry was furious with Cardinal Wolsey and the Church when the Pope refused the divorce.	☐	☐
c. Thomas Cranmer became the new Lord Chancellor of England, and Sir Thomas More became the new Archbishop of Canterbury.	☐	☐
d. The new Archbishop of Canterbury permitted Henry to divorce from Catherine and marry Anne Boleyn.	☐	☐
e. Princess Elizabeth was born in 1533 and Henry was very happy.	☐	☐
f. In 1534 Henry became the Supreme Head of the English Church.	☐	☐
g. In May 1536 Anne Boleyn was banished and Henry married Jane Seymour.	☐	☐
h. Jane Seymour gave birth to Prince Edward but died soon after.	☐	☐
i. Prince Edward received an excellent education from his father.	☐	☐

Choose the words from the Tudor rose to describe these people. Some words can be used more than once. Then choose two people and write a few sentences about them. Use your notebook if you don't have enough space.

patron of the arts

rich   great scholar

wore magnificent clothes   greedy

honest man   ambitious

opposed Henry's break with Rome

Lord Chancellor   was beheaded

organised a meeting in France

built palaces and castles

built Hampton Court

lived in luxury

Wolsey

....
....
....
....
....

More

....
....
....
....
....

Henry VIII

....
....
....
....
....

'All about Anne'

Are the following sentences right (R) or wrong (W)? If there isn't enough information to answer 'Right' or 'Wrong' choose 'Doesn't say' (DS).

a. Anne Boleyn was a young English lady of the court.
R ☐   **W** ☐   **DS** ☐

b. She was twenty-two years old.
R ☐   **W** ☐   **DS** ☐

c. She spoke Spanish very well.
R ☐   **W** ☐   **DS** ☐

d. Henry wanted to marry Anne and have a son with her.
R ☐   **W** ☐   **DS** ☐

e. She had six fingers on both hands.
R ☐   **W** ☐   **DS** ☐

f. She was imprisoned in the Tower of London and was beheaded.
R ☐   **W** ☐   **DS** ☐

g. Anne's father was a famous scholar.
R ☐   **W** ☐   **DS** ☐

Think about this – Witches and witchcraft

Anne Boleyn's enemies called her a witch because she had six fingers on her left hand. In ancient times people with physical defects were often called witches. Sometimes they were punished or killed.

a. Are witches part of the history of your country?

b. Do you believe in witches and magic?

c. How do you react to people who have a physical defect or handicap? ....
....

CHAPTER FOUR

Henry's Later Years

In Henry's time there were about 850 monasteries [1] in England and Wales. The religious orders [2] obeyed the Pope in Rome and not King Henry.

The monasteries had rich treasures and a quarter of all the land in England! Henry needed money so he and his Lord Chancellor, Cromwell, decided to close the monasteries and take their treasures and land.

Between 1536 and 1539 Cromwell sent his men to inspect them. When they returned they said, 'There is corruption [3] in the monasteries!' This was a good reason to close them.

Cromwell's men took the rich treasures and gave them to the King. They sent away the monks and nuns. [4] Some monasteries were destroyed and others were sold to the nobility. Many were transformed into beautiful houses. The land of the monasteries

---

1. **monasteries** : 修道院。
2. **religious orders** : 宗教團體。
3. **corruption** : 貪污。

4. **nuns** :

now belonged to King Henry, who became the richest monarch in Europe.

With the money from the monasteries, Henry built castles and fortifications [1] to protect the south coast of England. Deal Castle

Deal Castle.

in Kent was the biggest fort on the coast. It was built in the form of a rose, the Tudor symbol. Henry also built bigger warships. England now had the most powerful navy in Europe. (Henry's great warship the *Mary Rose* sank in 1545. In 1982 the remains of the ship were found, and now the *Mary Rose* can be seen at the Naval Dockyard in Portsmouth.)

Henry was now forty-eight. He was very fat and his health was not good. He became short-tempered [2] and oppressive. [3] Everyone had to obey him.

The Tudor court still attracted many artists and musicians. Hans Holbein the

Tudor symbol.

Younger was a great German artist. He was the King's royal painter. He painted many splendid pictures of the royal family and the Tudor court.

---

1. **fortifications** : 防禦工事。
2. **short-tempered** : 易發怒的。
3. **oppressive** : 暴虐的。

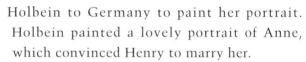

During the 1540s Henry built an extravagant new palace called Nonsuch Palace, in Surrey. A village was destroyed to build it, but it was never completed!

Henry's political position in Europe became weak. Spain and France wanted to destroy him. He needed a strong ally.[1]

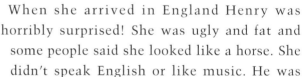

Cromwell convinced Henry to marry a German princess called Anne of Cleves. Henry sent Holbein to Germany to paint her portrait. Holbein painted a lovely portrait of Anne, which convinced Henry to marry her.

When she arrived in England Henry was horribly surprised! She was ugly and fat and some people said she looked like a horse. She didn't speak English or like music. He was

A gold coin from Tudor times.

very angry with Cromwell, who was accused of treason and beheaded in 1540. Henry married Anne for political reasons and divorced her seven months later in July.

Catherine Howard became Henry's fifth wife in the same month (July 1540). She was only nineteen years old and very frivolous.[2] Catherine was unfaithful and Henry became furious. She was accused of treason and beheaded in 1542.

At this point of his life Henry wanted a sincere companion and a nurse. He married his last wife, Catherine Parr, in 1543. She was a mature woman of thirty-one, who was gentle and well educated. (In Henry's time most people did not live past forty-five!)

---

1. **ally** : 盟國。
2. **frivolous** : 舉止輕浮的。

Catherine Parr, by unknown artist.
By courtesy of The National Portrait Gallery, London.

Catherine brought Henry's three children to court and took interest in their education. She was a kind and loving step-mother. [1] She also encouraged Henry to found Trinity College, a part of Oxford university. Henry's last marriage was successful.

During his later years there were wars with Scotland and France. These wars cost Henry an enormous amount of money. At last he made peace with France in 1546.

Henry's final years were tormented [2] by illness. He was obese. [3] He could not walk and was carried everywhere by servants. He had painful ulcers [4] on his legs, severe headaches and several other illnesses. Catherine Parr nursed [5] him patiently.

In his will [6] he named his three children heirs to the throne.

Henry remained a Catholic all his life. He died on 28 January 1547, and was buried at Windsor next to his third wife, Jane Seymour – the wife he loved the most.

---

1. **step-mother**：繼母。
2. **tormented**：受折磨。
3. **obese**：過度肥胖。
4. **ulcers**：潰瘍。
5. **nursed**：照顧。
6. **will**：遺囑。

UNDERSTANDING THE TEXT

 Circle the correct word.

a. There were approximately 850 *monks / monasteries* in England and *Wales / Scotland* in Henry's time.

b. Henry and *Cromwell / Cranmer* closed the monasteries and took their treasures and land.

c. Hans Holbein the *Elder / Younger* was the King's royal *musician / painter.*

d. Henry married the *German / French* Princess Anne of Cleves because he needed a *rich wife / strong ally.*

e. Henry's *fourth / fifth* queen was *Catherine Howard / Catherine Parr.* She was beheaded because she had *lovers / was fat and ugly.*

f. Henry's last *wife / nurse* was Catherine *Parr / Howard.*

g. In his later years Henry founded Trinity *Castle / College.*

h. During his last years Henry had several *illnesses / wives.* He could not *speak / walk* because he was obese.

i. Before his *marriage / death* in 1547 he named *his son Edward / three children* heir(s) to the throne.

 Match the name with the place.

name	place
a. Hans Holbein, the Younger	**1.** Portsmouth
b. Pope	**2.** Surrey
c. Deal Castle	**3.** Germany
d. 'Mary Rose'	**4.** Kent
e. Nonsuch Palace	**5.** Rome

3 Listen to the information more than once if necessary. Then fill in the family tree with the names and the birth dates.

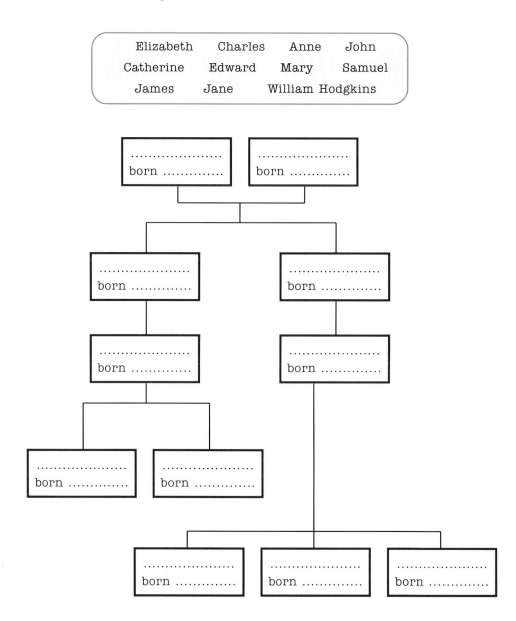

Elizabeth   Charles   Anne   John

Catherine   Edward   Mary   Samuel

James   Jane   William Hodgkins

....
born ....

....
born ....

....
born ....

....
born ....

....
born ....

....
born ....

....
born ....

....
born ....

....
born ....

....
born ....

....
born ....

Who are they?

Read the description of Henry's six wives and decide who they are.

a. I'm nineteen years old and very pretty. Henry thinks I'm frivolous. But he doesn't understand me. He's too old! I love another man – a young, handsome one. My name is:

☐ Anne of Cleves
☐ Catherine Howard
☐ Anne Boleyn

b. I've got black hair and dark eyes. I speak French and I'm very lively and intelligent. Henry wants to divorce his old wife and marry me! I want to give him a son. I'm:

☐ Anne Boleyn
☐ Jane Seymour
☐ Catherine Parr

c. I'm the step-mother of his three children. Henry is often oppressive and short-tempered, but I'm very patient. I nurse him and look after his children. My name is:

☐ Catherine of Aragon
☐ Catherine Howard
☐ Catherine Parr

d. Henry and I were happy together for many years. We have a lovely daughter. Now Henry doesn't love me anymore. He wants to divorce me and marry a woman who is a witch! What can I do? I'm:

☐ Jane Seymour
☐ Catherine of Aragon
☐ Anne of Cleves

e. I'm not beautiful and I'm fat, but I am a princess. I don't speak English and I don't like music. I don't understand why Henry divorced me! My name is:

☐ Jane Seymour
☐ Catherine Parr
☐ Anne of Cleves

f. When Henry met me he fell in love with me. We got married in 1536. I get along well with dear Henry because I'm a quiet, docile person. Soon I will give him a son. I'm his favourite wife. I'm:

☐ Jane Seymour

☐ Anne Boleyn

☐ Catherine Howard

5 **King Henry's wives**

What happened to them? Fill in the chart with the symbols below. Remember to fill in the missing names. One is done for you. The dates show when they were married to Henry VIII.

KEY   Children: **Ⓖ**=girl **B**=boy **N**=no children

Fate:[1] **D**=divorced **Ø**=died **X**=beheaded **S**=survived

Queen	Children	Fate
Catherine of Aragon (1509-1533)		
.... Boleyn (1533-1536)		
Jane .... (1536-1537)		
Anne .... (1540-1540)		
Catherine .... (1540-1542)		
.... Parr (1543-1547)		

---

1. **fate**：命運。

PART TWO

Elizabeth I when Princess, by unknown artist.
The Royal Collection © 1999, Her Majesty Queen Elizabeth II.

ELIZABETH I – THE VIRGIN QUEEN

INTRODUCTION

Queen Elizabeth's reign was so important in history that it was called the Elizabethan Age.

During her reign England's progress in the field of discovery and colonisation [1] was immense. Englishmen explored the New World and brought back an incredible [2] amount of riches. Trade began with other countries which helped to develop English commerce.

This was the beginning of the English colonisation in the New World.

The Elizabethan Age was also rich in learning. It was the age of Shakespeare, Bacon, Marlowe and other famous names.

Queen Elizabeth I was an exceptional [3] Queen. Like her father, Henry VIII, she was very intelligent and had a strong character. Unlike him, she was just and moderate. [4] Her people loved her greatly. She brought peace, unity and power to her country.

---

1. **colonisation**：建立殖民地。
2. **incredible**：難以置信的。
3. **exceptional**：非凡的。
4. **moderate**：溫和的。

Young Elizabeth

lizabeth was born on 7 September 1533. Her childhood was not happy. She was two years old when her mother, Anne Boleyn, was beheaded. She spent most of her early life at Hatfield House, away from her father, King Henry VIII.

However, Henry wanted his daughter to have the best education. Roger Ascham, a great scholar and humanist, [1] was Elizabeth's private teacher. She was very intelligent, witty [2] and enjoyed learning. She could read, write and speak Latin, Greek, French, Spanish, Italian and Welsh fluently. [3]

Elizabeth loved riding horses, hunting and dancing. Like her father, she had a talent for music and played the lute and the virginals. Unlike her father, she was very thrifty [4] and did not like spending money.

---

1. **humanist**：人文主義者。
2. **witty**：風趣的。
3. **fluently**：流利地。
4. **thrifty**：節儉的。

Elizabeth wasn't beautiful but she was elegant. She was thin, of medium height and very vain. [1] She had red hair, expressive eyes and lovely hands.

When Henry VIII died in 1547, Edward VI became King at the age of nine. But his reign was short. He died of tuberculosis [2] when he was only fifteen.

In 1553 his half-sister Mary (Catherine of Aragon's daughter) became Queen. Her mother was a Catholic and she wanted England to be a Catholic country again. Protestants were persecuted [3] and almost 300 were killed. For this reason she was also known as 'Bloody Mary'.

Young Elizabeth was in danger because she was a Protestant and was very popular with the people. Queen Mary thought Elizabeth plotted [4] against her and imprisoned her in the Tower of London in 1554. Elizabeth never forgot this terrible experience. After two months Mary freed her.

On the night of 17 November 1558 Queen Mary died. The bells of London rang and everyone celebrated: young Elizabeth was the new Queen!

Elizabeth became Queen at the age of 25. Like others of her time Elizabeth believed in astrology. [5] Her astrologer was John Dee, a famous astronomer. He chose the best day for her coronation ceremony: 15 January 1559.

Elizabeth was loved by the people but she was still in danger. The Kings of France and Spain wanted to invade England and bring back the Catholic faith.

---

1. **vain**：自視過高的。
2. **tuberculosis**：肺結核病。
3. **persecuted**：受迫害。
4. **plotted**：密謀。
5. **astrology**：占星術（又見頁**55**）。

Robert Dudley, Earl of Leicester, by unknown artist.
By courtesy of The National Portrait Gallery, London.

The young Queen was alert, clever and prudent. [1] She carefully chose advisers who were honest, loyal and experienced.

William Cecil was Elizabeth's Secretary of State [2] and her most important minister. He was her dear friend and she trusted him completely. Cecil served her for 40 years! Elizabeth was very wise to choose Matthew Parker as Archbishop [3] of Canterbury. He established a moderate Church of England and created a compromise [4] between Catholics and extreme Protestants.

She also chose Lord Robert Dudley to be part of her court. He was her childhood friend and sweetheart, and remained one of her favourites for many years.

Elizabeth was a strong ruler. England was now a Protestant country. The Act of Supremacy made her Head of the Church of England. All priests had to use the Book of Common Prayer.

The Queen liked meeting her people and was always kind to the old and the sick. She and her court frequently went on tours, or 'progresses', around the country to visit noble subjects. It was an honour to be part of a royal tour. However, the cost of entertaining [5] the Queen and her court was astronomical [6] and several nobles went bankrupt! [7]

---

1. **prudent** : 審慎的。
2. **Secretary of State** : 大臣。
3. **Archbishop** : 大主教。
4. **compromise** : 妥協。
5. **entertaining** : 娛樂。
6. **astronomical** : 龐大的。
7. **went bankrupt** : 破產。

UNDERSTANDING THE TEXT

 Fill in the gaps with the words in the tower.

advisers

William Cecil

intelligent

progresses

Elizabeth

imprisoned

loved

dancing   daughter

favourites   Tower

Protestants   alert

a. Young Elizabeth was very .... and enjoyed riding, hunting and ....

b. Catherine of Aragon's ...., Mary, became Queen and persecuted the ....

c. Queen Mary .... Elizabeth in the .... of London.

d. When Queen Mary died in 1558 .... became Queen of England and she was .... by the people.

e. Elizabeth was .... and clever, and chose her .... carefully.

f. .... was Elizabeth's most important minister. Lord Robert Dudley was one of her ....

g. The Queen liked meeting her people and often went on ....

Find the hidden word

Read the definitions and write the word.

a. very clever ＿ ＿|＿|＿ ＿ ＿ ＿ ＿ ＿ ＿

b. Roger Ascham was a ... ＿ ＿|＿|＿ ＿ ＿ ＿

c. musical instrument ＿ ＿|＿|＿ ＿ ＿ ＿ ＿

d. full of self-admiration ＿ ＿|＿|＿

e. religion ＿|＿ ＿ ＿ ＿

f. house where Elizabeth lived ＿ ＿|＿|＿ ＿ ＿ ＿ ＿

g. can be trusted ＿ ＿|＿|＿ ＿

Complete the following sentence with the word in the green column.

Queen Elizabeth was ＿ ＿ ＿ ＿ ＿ ＿ ＿ .

Now look up the opposite of this word.

 Question words

Read the answer then write the question using *why*, *who*, *when*, *what* and *where*.

a. .... was Elizabeth's mother?
Anne Boleyn.

b. .... did Queen Mary die?
She died in November 1558.

c. .... colour was Elizabeth's hair?
Her hair was red.

d. .... was young Elizabeth in danger?
Young Elizabeth was in danger because she was a Protestant.

e. .... was she imprisoned?
She was imprisoned in the Tower of London.

Think about this

a. Queen Mary and Queen Elizabeth were heads of state.

- How many other women do you know who were or are now heads of state?
- Do you think they are good rulers? Why? Why not?

b. Astrology is the study of how the sun, moon, stars and planets presumably influence people's lives.

Elizabeth believed in astrology and had her personal astrologer, John Dee.

- Is astrology popular today in your country?
- Do you think astrology can predict the future? Why? Why not?
- What is your astrological sign?
- Do you read your horoscope?
- Do you believe what it says?

CHAPTER TWO

Plots and Problems

Mary Stuart was Elizabeth's cousin and her most dangerous rival. [1] She was a Catholic and many Catholics wanted Mary to be the Queen of England. Mary was born in Scotland. She was the daughter of James V, King of Scotland and Mary Guise, a French noblewoman. Mary became Queen when she was only one week old. Since there were political problems in Scotland, Mary went to France at the age of five. She had a happy childhood in the luxurious French court. She married the French Dauphin [2] Francis and became Queen of France for a short time. In 1560 her husband, the young King of France, died and she returned to Scotland.

Scotland was a Protestant country but the Scots accepted her as their Queen. Mary was very beautiful, charming and fun-loving. [3] This worried Queen Elizabeth.

At this time something terrible happened: Elizabeth caught

---

1. **rival** : 競爭對手。
2. **Dauphin** : **1350-1830**年間的法國王太子。
3. **fun-loving** : 愛玩樂的。

smallpox, [1] a disease that killed many people in those days. She was dangerously ill for many days. Elizabeth's German doctor saved her life. Smallpox scars [2] remained on Elizabeth's face all her life. She always wore white powder and cosmetics to hide the scars.

Parliament wanted Elizabeth to marry as soon as possible. It was important to have an heir to the Tudor throne.

Several foreign monarchs wanted to marry Elizabeth: The Archduke of Austria, Ivan 'the Terrible' Tsar of Russia, the King of France and the King of Spain.

Many noblemen of her court wanted to marry her too. Sir Christopher Hatton loved her so much that he never married. However, Elizabeth spent most of her time with Robert Dudley, her favourite companion.

Mary Queen of Scots, by unknown artist. The Scottish National Portrait Gallery.

---

1. **smallpox**：天花病。
2. **scars**：疤痕。

Elizabeth was not interested in marriage. She feared that a foreign king was dangerous for England. And she did not want to divide her power with anyone.

In 1566, Robert Dudley, the Earl of Leicester, said, 'I really believe the Queen will never marry.' He was right. However, Parliament insisted. One day Elizabeth became angry and said, 'I

Execution of Mary Queen of Scots, by unknown artist.
The Scottish National Portrait Gallery.

am already bound unto [1] a husband, which is the kingdom of England!'

Elizabeth was afraid of a bad marriage. She had the example of her mother and of her cousin, Mary Stuart. After returning to Scotland, Mary married her cousin Lord Darnley in 1565. Soon after the marriage she hated him. Early in 1567 Darnley was killed. Many people suspected Mary and her lover, the Earl of Bothwell. When she married the Earl of Bothwell, the Scots were furious and she escaped to England.

Mary was now a real danger for the Queen – she was on English soil. [2] Catholic nobles began plotting against Elizabeth in favour of Mary. Elizabeth decided to imprison Mary in a remote [3] castle. She remained there for 19 years. Other plots against Elizabeth were discovered, but she didn't want to execute [4] her cousin. In 1586 Mary was finally accused of treason and in 1587 she was beheaded.

---

1. **bound unto**：（古語）嫁給。
2. **soil**：領土。
3. **remote**：偏遠的。
4. **execute**：處決。

UNDERSTANDING THE TEXT

1 **Are the following sentences true (T) or false (F)? Correct the false ones.**

		T	F
a.	Mary Stuart was a Protestant and became Queen of Scots.	☐	☐
b.	Mary was Elizabeth's biggest rival because many Catholics wanted her to be Queen of England.	☐	☐
c.	Elizabeth was dangerously ill with smallpox but a French doctor saved her life.	☐	☐
d.	Noblemen and monarchs wanted to marry Elizabeth, but she was not interested in marriage.	☐	☐
e.	The Scots suspected that Mary and Lord Darnley killed the Earl of Bothwell.	☐	☐
f.	Mary escaped to France and became a danger for Elizabeth.	☐	☐
g.	Catholic nobles plotted against Elizabeth in favour of Mary.	☐	☐
h.	Mary was imprisoned for 19 years and in 1587 was beheaded.	☐	☐

2 **Adjectives** (形容詞) **and nouns** (名詞)

Adjectives are often formed from nouns. Look at the example below. Go back to Chapter Two and match the correct noun with its adjective, or vice versa. The first is done for you.

NOUN	ADJECTIVE
happiness	...... happy ....
luxury	....
....	beautiful
anger	....
fury	....
....	dangerous

60

Now use the nouns or adjectives to complete the following sentences.

a. Mary Stuart was very .... in the ....
   French court.

b. Mary was charming and ....

c. The Scots were .... when Mary married the Earl
   of Bothwell.

d. Smallpox was a very .... disease.

e. Elizabeth became .... with Parliament.

3 The Catholic nobles who plotted against Elizabeth had a secret
code. They used it to write secret messages to Mary when she
was a prisoner. Below is an authentic message that Mary
received. Use the table to discover the secret message.

a	b	c	d	e	f	g	h	i	j	k	l	m
❋	⊙	✳	❄	✣	◆	✧	✳	✴	✪	☆	●	○

n	o	p	q	r	s	t	u	v	w	x	y	z
■	❏	☆	✳	▢	▲	▼	◆	✧	◗	✳	☆	▮

▼✳✣▢✣   ⊙✣   ▲✳✳   ■❏⊙●✣
✧✣■▼❏✣❏✣■   ◗✳❏   ◗✳●●   ◆■✳✣❏▼❋✳☆✣   ▼✳❋▼
✣✳✣✳◆▼✳❏■

Now fill in the gaps and write the message in modern English.

....
....

         S _ x   n _ b _ e   _ en _ le _ en   w _ _ l
              e _ ec _ te   _ ou.

61

Think about this

a. The rich Tudor family in the painting is eating fresh fruit after a meal.
Look at the children's fine clothes and the gold cup. Tudor families had many children although child mortality was very high. Disease was present in everyday life. It was caused by bad hygiene, poor diet and crowded homes. As you can see in the painting, there are two pets on the table: a bird and a small monkey. People in those times did not know about bacteria and that some animals carried diseases. About five out of ten babies died at birth. Families wanted several boys because they went to work and carried on the family name.
How many children are there in your family?

b. Smallpox was a terrible disease for many centuries. It killed millions of people. As a result of vaccination, smallpox does not exist anymore.
What modern day diseases are people afraid of? Is it possible to avoid these diseases?

c. Today we can live a longer and better life because we have vaccines, antibiotics and other medicines, but we also know how to take better care of ourselves.
Make a list of the things you automatically do that prevent catching diseases: e.g. washing fruit before eating it, etc.

William Brooke, 10th Lord Cobham and his Family, 1567 (panel);
by the Master of the Countess of Warwick.

Longleat House/Bridgeman Art Library.

CHAPTER THREE

Exploration and Discovery

n 1492 Christopher Columbus, an Italian navigator who sailed from Spain, discovered the New World. Now there were new countries to colonise. During the 1500s Spain and Portugal controlled sea travel on the Atlantic Ocean. England and other countries wanted to discover new trade routes to reach the Pacific Ocean. This was Elizabeth's biggest preoccupation and she sponsored many voyages.

Spain was the richest and most powerful country in Europe. Its empire extended to the West Indies, Central and South America. Spain and Portugal shared their treasures with the Pope in Rome.

The Spanish explorers took gold, silver, jewels and other riches from the natives and transported them to Spain on their galleons. Each galleon carried immense treasure.

Sir Francis Drake, by Gheeraerts, M. 1561 – 1635 (Style of).
National Maritime Museum, London.

Many Elizabethan captains and sailors were pirates, [1] but they were called 'privateers.' They had permission from the Queen to attack ships and take their treasure, which they divided with her! This was a common practice at that time.

Francis Drake, Sir John Hawkins and Thomas Cavendish were three famous privateers. Elizabeth affectionately called Drake 'my pirate.' Hawkins became the first Englishman to trade in African slaves.

Elizabeth asked Francis Drake, an expert navigator, [2] to sail across the South Atlantic, attack Spanish galleons [3] and take their treasure. She also wanted him to find new trade routes.

Drake left Plymouth in 1577 on his ship *The Golden Hind* and sailed South. He attacked several Spanish galleons on the South American coast. Then he sailed up the Pacific Coast and landed in northern California in 1579. He stayed there a month and claimed [4] California for Queen Elizabeth – today this place is called Drake's Bay, California, near San Francisco. In 1936 an old metal plate was found near Drake's Bay with these words on it:

BE IT KNOWN TO ALL MEN...
JUNE 17, 1579, BY THE GRACE OF GOD AND IN THE NAME OF
HER MAJESTY QUEEN ELIZABETH OF ENGLAND...
FOREVER I TAKE POSSESSION OF THIS KINGDOM...
TO BE KNOWN UNTO ALL MEN AS NOVA ALBION.

FRANCIS DRAKE

---

1. **pirates**：海盜。
2. **navigator**：航海家。
3. **galleons**：15-17世紀西班牙大帆船。
4. **claimed**：宣稱擁有。

Exploration and Discovery

(No one knows if this metal plate was Drake's or not.)

Drake then sailed across the Pacific Ocean and reached the East Indies. From there he sailed around the Cape of Good Hope and returned to England in 1580 after three long years.

Drake became the first Englishman to circumnavigate the globe. [1] His voyage is memorable [2] because he navigated in very difficult and dangerous conditions. He had no real maps.

Queen Elizabeth was extremely pleased with his results and knighted [3] him. She also gave him a special sword to use on England's enemies.

Drake did not only bring back immense treasures, he also brought back new foods and spices: pineapples, tomatoes,

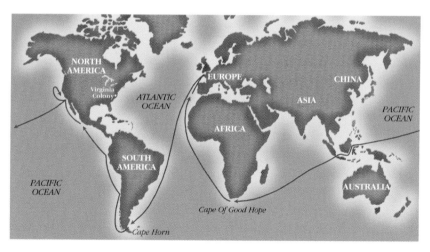

A map showing Drake's voyage, 1577 – 1580.

---

1. **circumnavigate the globe**：環繞地球航行。
2. **memorable**：值得紀念的。
3. **knighted**：冊封為爵士。

bananas, coconuts, peppers and chillies. [1] Spices were very important because they preserved [2] food and improved its taste.

English colonisation in North America began in 1584. Sir Walter Raleigh, a courageous soldier and explorer, was one of Elizabeth's favourites. He sailed to North America and set up the Virginia colony in honour of Elizabeth, the Virgin Queen.

Three years later 117 men, women and children arrived on Roanoke Island, in the Virginia colony. Living conditions were very difficult and many Indians were unfriendly. By 1590 the colony was abandoned. No one knew what happened to the colonists. [3]

Sir Walter Raleigh brought back potatoes and tobacco from the Virginia colony. He introduced pipe smoking to the Elizabethan court and it soon became popular. This was the beginning of the tobacco trade and industry.

---

1. **chillies** :
2. **preserved** : 保存。
3. **colonists** : 殖民地者。

UNDERSTANDING THE TEXT

 Choose the correct answer.

a. During the 1500s Spain was the most powerful country in Europe and
- [ ] many Spanish captains were pirates
- [ ] it controlled sea travel on the Pacific Ocean
- [ ] its empire extended to the West Indies, Central and South America

b. Spanish explorers
- [ ] took gold, jewels and other riches from the natives
- [ ] circumnavigated the globe
- [ ] sailed to North America to set up a colony

c. Three famous English privateers were
- [ ] Drake, Hawkins and Cavendish
- [ ] Drake, Raleigh and Cavendish
- [ ] Dudley, Hawkins and Raleigh

d. Elizabeth asked Sir Francis Drake to find new trade routes and
- [ ] set up the Virginia colony
- [ ] attack Spanish galleons and take their treasures
- [ ] find tobacco and potatoes

e. In 1579 Sir Francis Drake landed in northern California and
- [ ] found the tobacco plant
- [ ] set up the Roanoke colony
- [ ] claimed California for Queen Elizabeth

f. Drake circumnavigated the globe in three years and brought back
- [ ] treasure, new foods and spices
- [ ] African slaves
- [ ] a metal plate from California

g. In 1584 Sir Walter Raleigh
- [ ] became a privateer
- [ ] set up the Virginia colony in North America
- [ ] discovered Nova Albion

2 **Read the descriptions and write the number of the correct answer in the box.**

a. ☐ it is used for smoking   **1.** pineapple

b. ☐ it helps you find your way   **2.** spices

c. ☐ it was used to fight   **3.** silver

d. ☐ they preserve food   **4.** tobacco

e. ☐ an exotic fruit   **5.** sword

f. ☐ a precious grey metal   **6.** map

Match the letters with the numbers.
There are many words for pirates: privateers, corsairs, buccaneers, rovers, filibusters, etc!

a. ☐ What do pirates do?

b. ☐ What do they look like?

c. ☐ How can you recognise a pirate ship?

d. ☐ Name a well-known book whose characters include a pirate.

1. Look for the 'Jolly Roger', a black flag, with skulls, skeletons or crossbones on it.

2. They attack and rob ships at sea and they sometimes kill the crew!

3. *Treasure Island* (1883) by Robert Louis Stevenson.

4. In the past pirates wore long, dark jackets, colourful scarves and cotton shirts. Their trousers were wide and comfortable. Many pirates had a patch on one eye and a wooden leg!

3 Listen to this imaginary conversation between Queen Elizabeth and Sir Francis Drake. Then listen to it again and fill in the missing words.

ELIZABETH: Spain and Portugal .... sea travel on the Atlantic Ocean. This is a big .... We must find a .... trade route.

DRAKE: I am an expert navigator. I can sail .... the ocean and discover a new trade ....

ELIZABETH: I can .... for this important voyage. Take the .... men and the best .... This is a .... voyage. There are no ....

DRAKE: I am not ...., Your Majesty. I can explore the New .... and make maps. When must I ....?

ELIZABETH: In November of this .... Now listen carefully.

DRAKE: Yes, Your Majesty.

ELIZABETH: You must .... across the South Atlantic and .... the Spanish galleons. Then take .... treasure. Explore the oceans and .... new trade routes, new lands and new .... Keep a diary of .... you see.

DRAKE: I understand. It is an .... to serve my Queen.

CHAPTER FOUR

The Spanish Armada

England and Spain were enemies for many years. The King of Spain, Philip II, was angry with Elizabeth for several reasons: the religious conflict was a growing problem and Philip wanted to bring back the Catholic faith to England.

For many years English pirates and privateers attacked Spanish galleons and took their rich treasure. This exasperated Philip.

In 1585 Elizabeth sent an army to help Dutch Protestants fight the Spanish. When Mary Stuart was beheaded, Philip was furious. He decided to invade England and take the throne from Elizabeth. The Pope strongly supported his plan.

The Spanish Armada had about 130 big ships and about 28,000 men. It was commanded by the Duke of Medina Sidonia. Elizabeth knew about Philip's plan. She ordered her best captains, Sir Francis Drake, John Hawkins and Martin Frobisher to prepare for the attack.

The Spanish Armada

England had a powerful navy of about 160 smaller ships and about 14,000 men. It was commanded by Lord Howard of Effingham, one of Elizabeth's cousins.

In 1587 Drake attacked 30 Spanish galleons by surprise in Cadiz, Spain. 'I have singed[1] the King of Spain's beard,' he said proudly. His brilliant action pleased Elizabeth and hurt the Spanish.

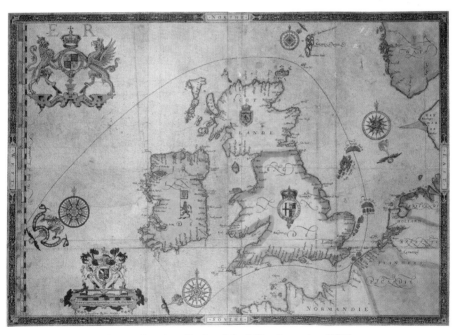

Chart showing the track[2] of the Armada, 1588,
by Rythier, Augustine after Adams, R.
National Maritime Museum, London.

---

1. **singed** : 燒焦。
2. **track** : 航線。

Elizabeth did not like war, but she was determined to defend England. Before the Spanish attack she visited her army and said,

Launch of Fireships Against the Armada, by Netherlandish School, 16th century. National Maritime Museum, London.

The Spanish Armada

'I have the body of a weak... woman, but I have the heart and stomach of a king!' She was a courageous woman.

In July 1588 the impressive Armada sailed up the English Channel. The weather was against the Spanish. The English attacked at Plymouth, using new tactics[1] to surprise the enemy. After several sea battles the Armada reached Calais (see map page 73).

Lord Howard sent eight fireships[2] to Calais. When the Spanish saw them they were terrified and immediately left the port. There were other sea battles and both countries fought courageously. In the end the Armada was badly defeated and returned to Spain with only 67 ships. This was a glorious victory for England, but it was a disaster for Spain. After this defeat, Spain slowly lost its sea power.

By 1590 Elizabeth was almost 60 years old. She was still healthy and energetic, but her aspect[3] changed. She wore a red wig[4] and her face was covered with heavy white make-up. Her teeth were in very bad condition. However, she was still vain. Every morning she spent more than two hours getting ready. She had about 3,000 magnificent dresses and innumerable[5] splendid jewels. She was always very careful with her personal hygiene and took a bath once a month. She hated bad odours and loud noise.

Elizabeth's court was a centre for playwrights,[6] artists and

---

1. **tactics** : 策略。
2. **fireships** : 用作攻敵着了火的船。
3. **aspect** : 容貌。
4. **wig** : 假髮。
5. **innumerable** : 無數的。
6. **playwrights** : 戲劇作家。

musicians. Edmund Spenser's famous work *The Faerie Queen* was dedicated to Elizabeth.

English drama flourished [1] during this period. William Shakespeare was born on 23 April 1564 in Stratford-upon-Avon. His father was a glove-maker. [2] He attended school at Stratford until he was fifteen.

William Shakespeare.

When he was eighteen he married Anne Hathaway and they had three children.

He went to London in about 1587, before the sea battle of the Spanish Armada. With England's brilliant victory over the Armada, the great English literary [3] Renaissance began and Shakespeare became the most famous English writer of all time.

In London he worked as an actor and began to write plays and poetry. By 1592 William Shakespeare was famous in London. His plays were very successful and he became a rich man. He wrote 38 tragedies, [4] comedies [5] and historical plays. [6] Some of his best known plays are *Hamlet, Macbeth, The Merchant of Venice, A Midsummer Night's Dream* and *Romeo and Juliet*. He and his group often performed for Queen Elizabeth and her court.

---

1. **flourished** : 興盛。
2. **glove-maker** : 手套製造者。
3. **literary** : 文學的。

4. **tragedies** : 悲劇。
5. **comedies** : 喜劇。
6. **historical plays** : 歷史劇。

People of all social classes started going to the theatre. In London open air theatres became very popular. Shakespeare's spectators were a noisy crowd. They talked, laughed, shouted, ate and drank during the performances. In open air theatres plays began in the afternoon when there was plenty of light. When it rained many of the spectators got wet. Women's roles[1] were played by young men, because women did not act in the theatre. Shakespeare's plays were performed at the Globe, the Swan and the Rose Theatres.

Shakespeare died on his birthday in 1616 and was buried in Stratford-upon-Avon. (The Globe Theatre was recently rebuilt so you can enjoy Shakespeare's plays on the original site in London.)

Other important Elizabethan playwrights were Ben Jonson and Christopher Marlowe.

Elizabeth's last favourite was the handsome Earl of Essex. She loved him dearly, although he was 34 years younger than her. She made him a military leader but he betrayed[2] her. He was accused of treason and beheaded in 1601.

In 1603 Elizabeth was 70 years old. She ate very little and was weak. She died on March 24, 1603, and was the last Tudor monarch. She named James VI of Scotland, the son of Mary Stuart, heir to the throne. Her people mourned her for a long time.

Her reign lasted 44 years. Under Elizabeth trade grew, Spain was defeated and England became a European power.[3]

---

1. **roles**：角色。
2. **betrayed**：出賣。
3. **power**：強國。

UNDERSTANDING THE TEXT

1 **Choose the correct answer.**

a. Who was angry with Queen Elizabeth?
- [ ] Edmund Spenser
- [ ] the Dutch Protestants
- [ ] King Philip of Spain

b. Who decided to invade England and take the throne from Elizabeth?
- [ ] Lord Howard of Effingham
- [ ] King Philip of Spain
- [ ] Duke Medina Sidonia

c. How many ships and men were there in the Spanish Armada?
- [ ] 130 ships and about 28,000 men
- [ ] 197 ships and about 15,000 men
- [ ] 183 ships and about 15,000 men

d. What terrified the Spanish in Calais?
- [ ] the English army
- [ ] eight fireships
- [ ] the powerful English navy

e. What happened to the Spanish Armada?
- [ ] it was victorious
- [ ] it was destroyed at Calais
- [ ] it was defeated

f. Who was the greatest English writer?
- [ ] William Shakespeare
- [ ] Ben Jonson
- [ ] Christopher Marlowe

g. The Globe, the Swan and the Rose were
- [ ] plays written by Shakespeare
- [ ] open-air theatres in London
- [ ] protagonists of a Shakespeare comedy

❷ Summary

Put the following sentences in chronological order. [1] One is done for you.

a. ☐ When Queen Mary died Elizabeth became Queen of England.

b. ☐1 Elizabeth was born in 1533 and was the daughter of Henry VIII and Anne Boleyn.

c. ☐ Elizabeth had several favourites but was not interested in marriage.

d. ☐ Sir Walter Raleigh set up the Virginia colony in North America in 1584.

e. ☐ Elizabeth's cousin, Mary Stuart, was a dangerous rival and was beheaded.

f. ☐ The English Navy defeated the Spanish Armada in 1588.

g. ☐ Elizabeth was a strong ruler and became the head of the Church of England.

h. ☐ In 1580 Sir Francis Drake circumnavigated the globe and brought back a lot of treasure and new foods.

i. ☐ When Elizabeth died in 1603 she named James VI of Scotland heir to the throne.

---

1. **chronological order**：按時間先後次序。

'Reading' a Painting

The Armada Portrait was painted to celebrate England's victory over the Spanish Armada in 1588. Smaller and faster ships were victorious over a powerful fleet of big galleons. The sea was England's best ally: many Spanish ships were destroyed by sea storms and tempests. In this painting two different moments of the sea battle can be seen in the background. A day scene represents the Spanish fleet advancing on a clear sea, confident of victory. The night scene shows the defeat of the Armada in the English Channel. In the foreground you can see Queen Elizabeth I. She was considered almost a divinity [1] by her people and her portraits are similar to holy [2] images. Her face is eternally [3] young and there are no shadows on it. Elizabeth controlled her own image. No painting or drawing representing her circulated [4] without her permission. This explains why in all her portraits she looks 'frozen' at more or less the same

---

1. **divinity** : 神明。
2. **holy** : 神聖的。
3. **eternally** : 永恒地。
4. **circulated** : 流傳。

age and never looks older. The Queen's magnificent gown is made of velvet and silk. It is decorated with pearls and gold. Every ribbon on her gown is decorated with a precious stone.

Elizabeth's hand is on the globe. Her fingers are touching the Americas, where Sir Walter Raleigh established the Virginia colony. He called it Virginia in honour of Queen Elizabeth, the Virgin Queen. A small statue of a sea creature is near her left hand. In this painting she is the ruler of both earth and sea. When you 'read' this portrait you can see that the Elizabethan painters were not interested in naturalism. [1] They did not depict [2] reality in their paintings, as artists did in the Italian Renaissance at that time (think of paintings by Leonardo, Raffaello and Michelangelo). The English painters preferred to use symbols and emblems [3] in their works.

---

1. **naturalism** : 自然主義風格。
2. **depict** : 繪畫出。
3. **emblems** : 標誌。

"The Armada Portrait" of Queen Elizabeth I,
by George Gower (c. 1588) Woburn Abbey.

By kind permission of the Marquess of Tavistock and the Trustees
of the Bedford Estate.

Look at the painting and answer the questions.

1. In the background there are two representations of the Armada. Which one shows the voyage and which one shows the defeat of the Spanish fleet?
   a. voyage ☐ the one to the left ☐ the one to the right
   b. defeat ☐ the one to the left ☐ the one to the right

2. Do you think the portrait
   a. represents Elizabeth as she really was?
   b. gives an idealised image of the Queen, according to the idea of beauty at the time?

3. The face of the Queen is
   a. happy   **b.** sad   **c.** without expression

4. Observe the colour of Elizabeth's face. It is
   a. dark (tanned) [1]
   b. very pale

5. Do you think it was fashionable for noble ladies to be tanned? Is it fashionable today?

6. On the left of the Queen there is
   a. a cat   **b.** a crown   **c.** a sword

7. What does the crown represent?
   a. poverty   **b.** kindness   **c.** royal power

8. The Queen's gown is
   a. precious and elegant
   b. comfortable to wear

9. The narrow waistline was obtained by wearing an iron corset. [2] Do women wear uncomfortable clothes today?

10. In those times, the faces of kings and queens could be reproduced only in paintings, engravings, [3] statues and coins. Today things are different. Can you recognise the face of the present monarch of England? Where have you seen it?

---

1. **tanned** : 曬黑的。   2. **corset** : 緊身內衣。   3. **engravings** : 刻板畫。

PART THREE

Queen Victoria (1875), by Heinrich von Angeli.
The Royal Collection © 1999, Her Majesty Queen Elizabeth II.

VICTORIA – MOTHER OF THE EMPIRE

INTRODUCTION

Queen Victoria reigned [1] longer than any other British Monarch: 63 years! She was an honest, highly dedicated monarch and was dearly loved by her people. During her reign Britain became the richest and most powerful nation in the world.

The Victorian Age was a time of great change in the way people lived and worked. The train replaced the stage-coach [2] and electricity was used for lights. It was also a time of exceptional achievements [3] in science and industry.

In other parts of the world photography, cars and telephones were invented. Victoria was the first monarch that was photographed.

Charles Dickens, Emily and Charlotte Brontë, Robert Louis Stevenson, Oscar Wilde and other great writers created their masterpieces [4] during the Victorian Age.

The British Empire grew and expanded around the world. It became so vast that 'the sun never set on it'.

Commerce and industry prospered, and created a lot of wealth. People moved from the country to industrial towns and cities to work in factories. This was the beginning of the Industrial Age.

---

1. **reigned** : 統治。
2. **stage-coach** :
3. **achievements** : 成就。
4. **masterpieces** : 傑作。

CHAPTER ONE

The Lonely Princess

O n 24 May 1819 a little princess was born at Kensington Palace in London. Her name was Alexandrina Victoria. She was the daughter of the Duke of Kent, King William's brother, and a German Princess, Victoria of Saxe-Coburg.

Victoria's father died when she was a baby. Her childhood was lonely and dull. She had no friends to play with. Her favourite toys were dolls. She rarely went out because her mother was very protective. She grew up with her mother and her strict [1] German governess, [2] Baroness Lehzen. Victoria adored Baroness Lehzen.

Victoria later wrote that she 'had no brothers or sisters to live with – never had a father, and did not know what a happy home life was.'

---

1. **strict** : 嚴厲的。
2. **governess** : （舊時）家庭女教師。

The young Princess loved animals and had three pets: a dog called Dash, a canary [1] and a parakeet. [2] She had private lessons in many subjects from half past nine in the morning to six in the evening. She loved singing and dancing.

At the age of twelve Victoria said, 'I see I am nearer the throne than I supposed.' On that day she made a promise, 'I will be good.'

When Victoria was 13 her mother decided that she must see Britain and that the British people must see her. The young Princess travelled to Wales, the Midlands, Yorkshire and the south coast. She was welcomed with enthusiasm everywhere.

These journeys were not a holiday but a part of her education.

Victoria wrote about her journey in her diary. She did not know that thousands of poor children worked in factories and mills [3] in terrible conditions. They never went to school and often died at a young age. She also learned that working people lived in small, dark houses and were often hungry.

On Victoria's seventeenth birthday her German cousin, Prince Albert, came to visit her. Victoria liked him immediately. Her mother thought Prince Albert was the ideal husband and Victoria agreed!

At five in the morning on 20 June 1837 Victoria received the news: King William IV died that night and she was now the Queen! She was only eighteen and knew very little about government or politics. At half past eleven that morning she went

---

1. **canary** : 金絲雀。

2. **parakeet** :

3. **mills** : 織造及鋼鐵工廠。

to meet her advisers, the Privy Councillors. [1] She spoke and behaved calmly, and everyone admired her.

The young Queen now lived at Buckingham Palace, away from the strict control of her mother. Victoria enjoyed going to the opera and the ballet, and began horse riding. Since she was short (almost 5 foot = 1.5 metres) she felt taller on a horse!

Lord Melbourne, the Prime Minister, was the most important person in Victoria's early years as Queen. He was a kind and loyal friend. He gave her advice and helped her understand politics and government.

In 1839 Victoria's cousin, Albert, visited her again. This is what she wrote in her diary: 'Albert really is quite charming, and so excessively handsome. My heart is quite going.' [2] Victoria loved Albert and proposed to him! (Albert could not propose because he was of lower rank.)

An 1837 handbill asking Londoners to celebrate Victoria's 18th birthday.

---

1. **Privy Councillors**：作為國王顧問的樞密院官員。
2. **quite going**：心跳急速。

They were married in 1840. Victoria and Albert loved each other very much. She called him 'an angel.' However, Albert was a foreigner and not everyone liked him. Parliament did not give Albert a title and many Londoners said rude things about him.

Albert was intelligent, well-educated and responsible. He was very interested in science, music and the arts. Victoria learned from Albert to be a dedicated monarch. The Queen asked for his help on government affairs and they always worked together.

Queen Victoria and Prince Albert, 30th June 1854.
The Royal Archives © 1999, Her Majesty Queen Elizabeth II.

UNDERSTANDING THE TEXT

 1 Listen to the sentences and circle the correct word.

a. Victoria's childhood was *lively / lonely*. She grew up with her *mother / father* and her German *governor / governess*.

b. When Victoria was *30 / 13* she visited *parts / past* of Britain, and *wrote / rode* about her journey in her *dairy / diary*.

c. Victoria *became / becomes* Queen when she was 18 *years / ears* old.

d. Lord Melbourne helped Victoria *understanding / understand* politics and *governor / government*.

e. Victoria loved Albert and *day / they* were *marry / married* in February 1840.

f. Not everyone liked Albert *because / became* he was a *foreign / foreigner*.

g. Albert was *negligent / intelligent* and responsible. Victoria learned from *him / his* to be a *delicate / dedicated* monarch.

 2 Adverbs of frequency (頻度副詞)**: always, usually, often, sometimes, never, just**

Look at this sentence:

They never went to school and often died at a young age.

Never and **often** are adverbs of frequency. Adverbs of frequency answer the question *How often ...?* They are positioned after the verb 'to be' but just before the other verbs or just after the first auxiliary verb (助動詞):

I am always late.

I will always love you.

I have just been listening to Gilbert and Sullivan.

Read the chart and tick the correct adverb of frequency.
How often do you ...?

	always	usually	often	sometimes	never
play tennis	☐	☐	☐	☐	☐
go to the disco	☐	☐	☐	☐	☐
eat breakfast	☐	☐	☐	☐	☐
prepare dinner	☐	☐	☐	☐	☐
go to a rock concert	☐	☐	☐	☐	☐
watch TV	☐	☐	☐	☐	☐
play with the computer	☐	☐	☐	☐	☐
see your friends	☐	☐	☐	☐	☐
clean your room	☐	☐	☐	☐	☐
get dressed	☐	☐	☐	☐	☐
go to the cinema	☐	☐	☐	☐	☐
take the bus	☐	☐	☐	☐	☐

How often are you ...?

happy ....

hungry ....

sad ....

angry ....

nervous ....

afraid ....

sleepy ....

3 Now use the chart to interview a friend.

Start with: How often do you ...? Do you ever ...? or
Are you often ...? Are you ever ...?

Here is page from young Victoria's diary. Unscramble the words and put the verbs in the Past Simple.

Midlands, April 15, 1832

This *nrgmoin* I (visit) .... a town with a *gbi* factory. I (be) .... very *sdupsreir*!
I (see) .... small, dark *suehos* and dirty *etestrs*. A *myafli* of eight people (live) .... in *neo* room! They (be) .... very *orpo*, hungry and *dsa*.
Then I (go) .... to see the *yatcofr*. *Yamn* children (work) .... there. They (do) .... dangerous *rwok*. They (do) .... not have any shoes on their *tefe* and it (be) .... very cold.
There (be) .... no *hoscol* in the town. What a sad *yad*!

 Think about this

In the past parents decided who their children married. These were called 'arranged marriages'. Young people were not free to decide. This created a lot of problems because love was not the most important part of marriage.

Many royal marriages were decided when the children were still young. These were marriages of political convenience. Do you remember why Henry VIII married Anne of Cleves?

Do you know the tragic love story of 'Romeo and Juliet' by William Shakespeare? Juliet Capulet loved Romeo Montague, but their families hated each other. Juliet could not marry Romeo because her parents had arranged a marriage with Paris, a rich nobleman. We all know what happened in the end. Even today, 'arranged marriages' are common in many cultures around the world.

a. Why was Victoria's marriage to Albert so special?

b. What do you think of 'arranged marriages'?

c. Do you ask your parents' opinion about your boyfriend/girlfriend?

d. Do you think parents can give their opinion about their son's or daughter's wife or husband?

CHAPTER TWO

The Growth of Commerce and Industry

I n November 1840 the Queen had her first child, Victoria. She was very clever and was the Queen's favourite child. In 1841 Albert Edward, Prince of Wales, was born.

Between 1840 and 1857 Victoria and Albert had nine children – four sons and five daughters. Victoria was a strict mother. The children's food and clothing were always very simple. Victoria and Albert were devoted parents and spent a lot of time with their children. Family values [1] and morality [2] were very important to the royal couple. They became an example for their people. Most Victorians had large families. In the late 1800s, the average family had five or six children.

Albert introduced the first Christmas tree to the royal family,

---

1. **values**：價值觀。
2. **morality**：道德。

since it was a German custom. Soon it was popular all over Britain. Victoria was very fond of Christmas and its traditions.

The first public railway opened in 1825 and attracted a lot of attention. It was built by George Stephenson, an engineer. In 1830 the Liverpool to Manchester Railway opened and soon transported 1,200 passengers every day.

With the railway, people and goods travelled cheaply and quickly. Railways spread [1] rapidly all over England, Scotland and Wales. People started going to the seaside and seaside towns developed. By 1848 there were no more stage coaches – almost everyone travelled by train.

The Royal Family at Osborne, May 1857.
The Royal Archives © 1999, Her Majesty Queen Elizabeth II.

---

1. **spread** : 伸展。

In 1842 Victoria and Albert took their first train ride. The Queen liked the speed, comfort and privacy of the train. Soon the royal family travelled by Royal Train, a specially designed carriage. In 1840 the first national postal system was created and the 'Penny Black' became the first adhesive [1] postage stamp. Victoria's profile [2] appeared on it. It cost only one penny to send a letter anywhere in Great Britain. Today the red Victorian letter boxes are still used!

Victoria had three royal houses but she didn't like any of them. She wanted a private, remote family home. She and Albert bought a large estate [3] called Osborne on the Isle of Wight. Victoria loved Osborne and was very happy there.

In 1847 the royal couple bought a house in Scotland: Balmoral Castle. It was surrounded by green hills and forests. Victoria liked the fresh, clean air and Albert liked hunting and fishing.

Poverty was a big problem in 19th-century Britain. Working people had a very difficult life. Adults and children worked long hours in factories in dangerous conditions. They were usually hungry and often ill. Squalid [4] houses, unclean water and dirty streets caused many diseases. The air was full of smoke and fog. People did not live long in these conditions.

People without work lived on the streets. They were beggars [5] or thieves. Others lived in workhouses. [6] Some Victorians tried to help

---

1. **adhesive**：黏膠的。
2. **profile**：側面輪廓。
3. **estate**：莊園。
4. **squalid**：骯髒的。
5. **beggars**：乞丐。
6. **workhouses**：（舊時）貧民庇護工場。

the poor. Dr Barnardo opened a home for orphans in London. Charles Dickens wrote about these social problems in his novels, for example in *Oliver Twist* and *David Copperfield*.

Social reforms were seriously needed. In 1847 the Ten Hour Act limited the working day of women and children to ten hours a day!

In 1848 Parliament passed laws to make towns and cities cleaner. But progress was very slow.

The middle and upper classes had clean, comfortable houses, far from the industrial centres in green areas called

Children at work.

suburbs. Their children received a good education.

Under Victoria's reign Britain became the richest commercial nation. It produced machines, textiles, ships and other goods, and sold them to other countries.

Albert wanted to show Britain's products, inventions and machines to the world. He decided to open an international exhibition. For two years he worked intensely on this complex project. The British began to appreciate Albert's qualities.

On 1 May 1851 Queen Victoria opened the Great Exhibition in the Crystal Palace in London. She called it 'the most beautiful spectacle ever seen.' The Crystal Palace was truly a spectacle. It

was made of iron and glass, and was as big as four football fields! There were over 7,000 exhibitors from Britain and 6,000 from

The Inauguration of the Great Exhibition, 1 May 1851,
by David Roberts (1796 – 1864).
The Royal Collection © 1999, Her Majesty Queen Elizabeth II.

other countries. It was an enormous success with over 6 million visitors in 140 days!

UNDERSTANDING THE TEXT

1 **Are the following sentences true (T) or false(F)? Correct the false ones.**

	T	F
a. Victoria and Albert had nine children but they spent little time with them.	☐	☐
b. People liked the railway because it was fast and cheap.	☐	☐
c. The Penny Black was the name of the first public railway.	☐	☐
d. Osborne and Balmoral Castle were the royal couple's favourite homes.	☐	☐
e. Working people lived and worked in very difficult conditions during the nineteenth century.	☐	☐
f. Charles Dickens wrote about the social problems of the Victorian Age in his novels.	☐	☐
g. The Ten Hour Act of 1847 made education free for everyone.	☐	☐
h. Britain became the richest commercial nation under Victoria's reign. It produced machines, textiles and ships, and sold them to other countries.	☐	☐
i. There were more than 13,000 exhibitors at the Great Exhibition in London.	☐	☐

Crossword puzzle

Across

1. The streets of London were full of ... and fog.

2.

3.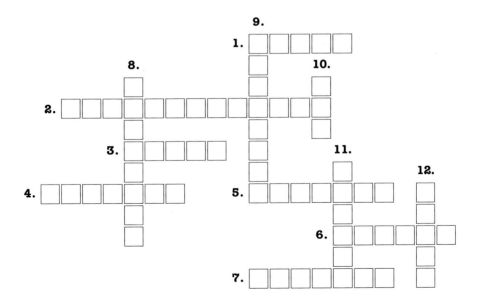

4. Victoria's estate on the Isle of Wight.

5. Victorian writer.

6. Prince Albert was ... .

7. Green areas far from the city.

Down

8. The Queen's first child.

9. Balmoral Castle is in ... .

10. Victorian letter boxes are ... .

11. Poor person who asks for food or money.

12. The Great Exhibition was made of iron and ... .

Look it up!

During the Industrial Revolution of the late 18th century, many people in Britain went to the cities and towns to work in the factories and mills.

In your country ...

a. when did the Industrial Revolution begin?

b. did people go to the cities and towns to work? Where did they go?

c. how did they live?

d. when was the first railway built?

e. which cities are industrial centres today?

 Match the letters with the numbers.

a. posh	**1.**	post office box
b. p.m.	**2.**	Peninsular and Oriental shipping company
c. P&O		
d. PR	**3.**	post meridian; afternoon
e. P.O. box	**4.**	luxurious
	5.	public relations

CHAPTER THREE

Wars and Loss

During the 1850s there were wars and revolts [1] in Europe and Asia. British soldiers fought in several of them. The most important was the Crimean War on the Black Sea. Russia wanted to expand its empire and perhaps block the Mediterranean and overland routes to India. So Britain and France decided to help Turkey fight Russia.

The Crimean War was the first war that was photographed. For the first time newspapers showed photographs of a war – a painful, tragic spectacle. [2]

Victoria was very unhappy because the soldiers suffered. She sent them mittens [3] and scarves, and visited the wounded [4] soldiers in British hospitals. She wrote letters to the soldiers' widows. Albert wrote hundreds of letters to Members of

---

1. **revolts** : 叛亂。

2. **tragic spectacle** : 悲慘景象。

3. **mittens** :

4. **wounded** : 受傷的。

Parliament to ask them to send more help to the soldiers.

Victoria helped Florence Nightingale [1] who went to Crimea with 38 nurses. She courageously set up a hospital for wounded soldiers and saved many lives. After the war Florence Nightingale opened the first school for nurses in London. This was the beginning of modern nursing and improved hygienic conditions in hospitals.

When the Crimean War ended in 1856 Victoria presented a special medal for courage to many soldiers. This medal was called the Victoria Cross and it was made of captured Russian cannon!

At this time India was controlled by the British East India Company, a trading company set up in India. In 1857 there was a rebellion [2] against the British who lived

Victoria Cross.

in India. It was called the Indian Mutiny. [3] Thousands of people were killed. After this rebellion India became part of the British Empire and was controlled by the British government.

Victoria was very healthy and was rarely ill. She did not like hot rooms and always kept windows open, even in winter!

Albert was usually cold and was not as healthy as Victoria. He worked too much and rarely rested. He was also worried about his son, the Prince of Wales. The Prince's adventures [4] with women and

---

1. **Florence Nightingale**：護士行業創始人 南丁格爾（**1820-1910**）。
2. **rebellion**：叛變。
3. **mutiny**：兵變。
4. **adventures**：刺激活動。

gambling shocked Albert, who was very upright. [1]

Albert became very tired and weak. In November 1861 he caught typhoid fever, [2] but he continued working until he died on 14 December. Victoria was devastated – it was the greatest agony [3] of her life. She was lost without Albert. She was convinced that her son, the Prince of Wales, was responsible for Albert's death. She did not permit the Prince of Wales to help her with government work.

Victoria visited Albert's impressive tomb at Frogmore near Windsor regularly. She wanted everyone to remember him. The Albert Memorial and the Royal Albert Hall near the Kensington Gardens in London were built to honour her beloved husband.

In her sadness and misery Victoria became a recluse. [4] For thirteen years she refused to appear in public and go to Privy Council meetings. However, she continued studying government papers privately and never lost contact with her kingdom. She spent a lot of time at Balmoral Castle, far from

The Albert Memorial, London.

---

1. **upright** : 正直。
2. **typhoid fever** : 傷寒病。
3. **agony** : 極大痛苦。
4. **recluse** : 隱居者。

London. A Scottish servant called John Brown became her loyal friend.

During this period Victoria and the monarchy became very unpopular, and some politicians wanted to abolish it and create a republic!

Queen Victoria on Fyrie, attended by J. Brown (left)
and J. Grant, Balmoral, October 1863.

The Royal Archives © 1999, Her Majesty Queen Elizabeth II.

UNDERSTANDING THE TEXT

1 Choose the correct answer.

a. During the Crimean War, Britain and France
- [ ] helped Turkey to fight Russia
- [ ] expanded their empires
- [ ] fought against India

b. After the Crimean War Florence Nightingale
- [ ] opened a hospital in London
- [ ] opened the first school for nurses
- [ ] became a doctor

c. The Victoria Cross was
- [ ] an impressive monument in Windsor
- [ ] a special medal for courage at war
- [ ] the name of Florence Nightingale's hospital in Crimea

d. After the Indian Mutiny of 1857
- [ ] the British East India Company left India
- [ ] India became an independent nation
- [ ] India became part of the British Empire

e. Albert was not as healthy as Victoria and in November 1861 he
- [ ] caught typhoid fever and died in December
- [ ] went to live in Scotland
- [ ] consulted several German doctors

f. Victoria was devastated by Albert's death and
- [ ] became very ill
- [ ] went to live at Frogmore near Windsor
- [ ] became a recluse

g. During this period some politicians wanted
- [ ] to abolish the monarchy and create a republic
- [ ] a new Queen
- [ ] a new Prime Minister

2 Who did what?

Who:

a. was very upright? ....

b. liked gambling? ....

c. wrote letters to the soldiers' widows? ....

d. went to Crimea with 38 nurses? ....

e. received the Victoria Cross? ....

f. was Victoria's loyal friend at Balmoral Castle? ....

g. wanted to abolish the monarchy? ....

h. was rarely ill? ....

i. died of typhoid fever? ....

j. opened the first school for nurses in London? ....
....

3 Go back to Chapter Three and underline all the words that talk about sadness and suffering.

Now write them here: ....
....

Use these words to create sentences about the following:

a. War is ....

b. The wounded soldiers ....

c. When Prince Albert died, Victoria was ....

CHAPTER FOUR

The End of an Era

In 1866 Victoria opened Parliament for the first time after Albert's death. She was dressed in black, the colour of mourning, which she wore for the rest of her life.

Transportation became a big problem in London because roads were always crowded. In 1863 the first underground railway in the world opened in London. Today it is called the 'tube'.

This was a period of social reforms.[1] In 1870 the Education Act was passed. It introduced the first state schools for all children between the ages of five and thirteen.

Factory reforms, new laws for the poor and new hospitals improved people's lives. In 1875 many slums[2] were destroyed and better homes were built. However, poverty[3] was still a big problem.

---

1. **social reforms**: 社會改革。
2. **slums** : 貧民窟。
3. **poverty** : 貧窮。

The poor people of London.

In 1878 the American inventor Alexander Bell showed the Queen his invention, the telephone.

Victoria was astonished![1] She was even more astonished to learn about the invention of a new means of transport: the automobile.

This was a period of revolutionary change.

At this time Victoria's favourite Prime Minister was Benjamin Disraeli, a witty, intelligent man. He got along well with[2] the Queen and encouraged her to return to public life.

Disraeli wanted to expand the British Empire. His political rival, William Gladstone, wanted to limit it. Victoria did not like Gladstone. He complained about the cost of the Albert Memorial.

Victoria liked Disraeli's idea of a bigger and stronger British Empire. In 1869 the Suez Canal, built by the French, opened and created an important trade route to India and

---

1. **astonished**：驚訝。
2. **got along well with**：與人相處融洽。

the East. Great Britain bought shares [1] in the canal to secure Britain's power in the East.

India was an important colony with its production of tea, silk and cotton. Victoria was fascinated by India and was delighted to become Empress of India in 1876. The British Empire expanded rapidly with the addition of Borneo, Burma and New Guinea. (see map on page 113)

David Livingstone was a British missionary and a great explorer. In the 1850s he travelled extensively [2] in Africa and made the first maps of Central Africa. He discovered six lakes, rivers, mountains and the biggest waterfall in

Benjamin Disraeli.

the world: called Victoria Falls in honour of the Queen. Henry Morton Stanley explored Lake Tanganyika and the Congo River.

In the 1880s Britain took control of large parts of Africa: Egypt, Nigeria, Kenya and Uganda. In 1883 there was a war in Sudan and rebels destroyed the British command [3] in Khartoum. From its African colonies Britain got cocoa, coffee and diamonds.

On 20 June 1887 Victoria celebrated her 50 years as Queen. The following day she rode through London in an open carriage [4]

---

1. **shares** : 股份。

2. **extensively** : 廣闊地。

3. **command** : 部隊。

4. **carriage** :

Great English Monarchs and their Times

for the spectacular [1] Golden Jubilee [2] celebrations. The streets were full of cheering people.

A procession of royal guests from all over the world rode in front of Victoria. There were Kings and Queens from Europe, the Crown Prince [3] of Prussia and Princes from India, Japan and Siam. Victoria was very fond of music and liked singing arias [4] from the comic operas of Gilbert and Sullivan. *The Mikado, The Pirates of Penzance* and *HMS Pinafore* are their most famous

Escort of Indian Cavalry passing the Houses of Parliament, June 22nd 1897.
The Royal Archives © 1999, Her Majesty Queen Elizabeth II.

1. **spectacular**：壯觀的。
2. **golden jubilee**：金禧（**50**週年）。
3. **crown prince**：王儲。
4. **arias**：歌劇中的詠嘆調。

operas. However, it was the famous British composer Edward Elgar who wrote music for the great celebration.

But Victoria felt sad and lonely. 'I sat alone,' she wrote, 'Oh! without my beloved husband!' All of her children married into royal families in different parts of Europe.

When Victoria celebrated her Diamond Jubilee in 1897 there was another gigantic procession, with 50,000 troops from all over the British Empire. On that day Victoria pressed a button to send a telegraph message around the empire: 'From my heart I thank my beloved people. May God bless them!'

In 1899 the British Empire was the biggest empire in the world.

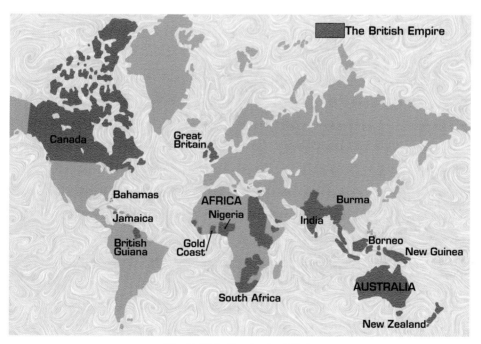

The British Empire in 1899.

It covered one-fifth of the earth's land area with 370 million people! (see map page 113)

Victoria was now an old woman and suffered from rheumatism. [1] She could not walk well but was still active. She worked from half past seven in the morning until late at night, studying government papers. She loved her people and her empire.

At the beginning of 1901 the Queen was very weak. On 22 January 1901 Victoria died at the age of 82 at Osborne House. Thousands of people wept during her funeral procession. [2] She was considered the Mother of the British Empire. She was buried beside her beloved Albert at Frogmore near Windsor.

Queen Victoria, c. 1882.
The Royal Archives © 1999, Her Majesty Queen Elizabeth II.

---

1. **rheumatism**：風濕病。
2. **funeral procession**：葬禮巡行。

UNDERSTANDING THE TEXT

 1 **Fill in the gaps with the words in the box.**

> India   diamonds   'tube'   automobile
>
> missionary   telephone   railway
>
> coffee   land   Disraeli   expand
>
> Golden Jubilee   Africa   social reforms
>
> Suez Canal   biggest   Empress

a. The .... in London was the first underground .... in the world.

b. In the 1870's there were several .... to help the poor.

c. Victoria was astonished by the invention of the .... and the ....

d. Victoria got along well with ...., who wanted to .... the British Empire.

e. The British government bought control of the ...., which opened an important trade route to ....

f. In 1876 Victoria became .... of India and the British Empire expanded rapidly.

g. David Livingstone was a British .... and explorer who made maps of ....

h. Britain got cocoa, ... and .... from Africa.

i. There were kings and queens from all over the world at Victoria's ....

j. In 1899 the British Empire was the .... empire in the world and covered one-fifth of the earth's .... area.

Find the names of the important people in Chapter Four and put them in the correct category. Then add any more you know from that period.

Politicians	Explorers	Inventors	Musicians

What did the explorers explore? ....
What did the inventors invent? ....
What did the musicians compose? ....
Can you name another invention of the 19th century? ....

 Look at the map of the British Empire on page 113. Make a list of the British colonies. Use an atlas to help you, if necessary.

Was your country part of the British Empire?
Where is English spoken in the world today?
Colour the English speaking countries in your favourite colour.

Think about this

a. Name five important inventions of the 20th century and say why they are important.
b. The 20th century was a time of space exploration. Name one space explorer.
c. In your opinion, what was the most important invention of the 19th century? And what about the 20th century? Why?
d. Can you predict an important invention of the 21st century?

EXIT TEST

CONTEXT

1 **Fill in the gaps with the correct words from the box.**

queen   Sir Francis Drake   treasures   Shakespeare   writer
monasteries   wives   beheaded   rival   English Church   daughter
Renaissance   heir   moderate   defeated   colony   intelligent

a. During King Henry's reign the .... developed in England.

b. King Henry had six .... and desperately wanted an .... to the Tudor throne.

c. Henry became the Supreme Head of the ....

d. Between 1536 and 1539 King Henry and Cromwell closed the .... in England and Wales and took their land and ....

e. Elizabeth was the .... of King Henry and Anne Boleyn. She became .... in 1558 and was an .... and .... monarch.

f. Mary Queen of Scots was Elizabeth's biggest .... She was .... in 1587.

g. During Elizabeth's reign .... circumnavigated the globe and Sir Walter Raleigh set up a .... in Virginia.

h. The Spanish Armada was .... by the powerful English navy in 1588.

i. In London .... wrote his famous plays and became the most famous English .... of all time.

117

COMPREHENSION

2 **Are the following sentences true (T) or false (F)? Correct the false sentences.**

	T	F
a. Henry VIII became King in 1509.	☐	☐
b. Henry VIII had five wives.	☐	☐
c. During the reign of Henry VIII, the Renaissance developed in England.	☐	☐
d. Henry VIII had four children by Jane Seymour.	☐	☐
e. Elizabeth I was a weak ruler.	☐	☐
f. During the reign of Elizabeth I, Francis Drake became the first Englishman to circumnavigate the globe.	☐	☐
g. Sir Walter Raleigh set up the Elizabeth colony in North America.	☐	☐
h. Elizabeth I's reign lasted 34 years.	☐	☐
i. Victoria became queen when she was only twenty years old and Benjamin Disraeli helped her understand politics and government.	☐	☐
j. Victoria loved Prince Albert dearly and they always worked together.	☐	☐
k. The Victorian Age was not a period of change.	☐	☐
l. Poverty was a big problem in 19th-century Britain.	☐	☐
m. The Suez Canal opened an important trade route to the West.	☐	☐

- **Name some inventions of the 19th century.**
- **Who explored Africa during Queen Victoria's reign?**

GRAMMAR

3 **Fill in the gaps with the correct adjectives formed by the nouns in the first column.**

NOUNS	ADJECTIVES
danger	
courage	
success	
happiness	
beauty	
anger	
luxury	
fury	
health	

PET

4 **Read the text and choose the correct word (A, B, C or D) for each space.**

Henry VIII became king just ¹......................... his eighteenth
birthday. He was married to Catherine of Aragon for almost
²...................... years and had one daughter, Mary. Henry then
married Anne Boleyn and had another daughter, Elizabeth. He
finally had a surviving son, Edward, with his ³......................... wife,
Jane Seymour.

During his reign came the beginning of the Reformation and the
Protestant Church. Henry and Cromwell, his Lord Chancellor, also
closed the ⁴......................... and took their treasures and land.
Henry married three more times and died in 1547.

Elizabeth I became Queen in 1559. She was a strong ruler, but her
⁵......................., Mary Stuart, was her most dangerous rival. Mary
was later accused of treason and was beheaded.

During Elizabeth I's reign Sir Francis Drake circumnavigated the
globe. He claimed California for Queen Elizabeth and from his voyage

he brought back new 6........................ and spices as well as immense treasures.

In 1588 the English Navy defeated the Spanish Armada bringing a great victory for 7........................ . William Shakespeare became the most famous 8........................ during Elizabeth I's reign.

Elizabeth never married and died in 1603. She was the last Tudor monarch.

Victoria became Queen in 1837 at the age of eighteen. She married her German cousin, Albert, in 1839. They had 9........................ children. Albert introduced the first Christmas 10........................ to the royal family.

The Victorian Age was a period of great social and industrial change. The first public railway opened in 1825. Britain became the 11........................ commercial nation. India became part of the British 12........................ .

Victoria was devastated when Albert died. However, her reign continued to see social and industrial progress. The 'Mother of the British Empire' died in 1901, having reigned for 63 years!

1. **A** after   **B** at   **C** before   **D** during

2. **A** twenty   **B** ten   **C** fifteen   **D** two

3. **A** fourth   **B** second   **C** fifth   **D** third

4. **A** schools   **B** churches   **C** monasteries   **D** castles

5. **A** sister   **B** daughter   **C** mother   **D** cousin

6. **A** plants   **B** foods   **C** flowers   **D** drinks

7. **A** France   **B** Spain   **C** Italy   **D** England

8. **A** painter   **B** writer   **C** musician   **D** architect

9. **A** seven   **B** eight   **C** nine   **D** ten

10. **A** dinner   **B** pudding   **C** decorations   **D** tree

11. **A** poorest   **B** weakest   **C** smallest   **D** richest

12. **A** Empire   **B** Isles   **C** Cross   **D** State

PET

5 **You are completing a questionnaire.**
Look at the form and answer each question.

A. Name: Henry VIII

    Year of coronation: 1..............................

    Married – yes or no?   2..............................

    Number of surviving children: 3..............................

    Year of death: 4..............................

B. Name: Elizabeth I

    Year of coronation: 1..............................

    Married – yes or no?   2..............................

    Number of surviving children: 3..............................

    Year of death: 4..............................

C. Name: Victoria

    Year of coronation: 1..............................

    Married – yes or no?   2..............................

    Number of surviving children: 3..............................

    Year of death: 4..............................

6 **Write a few sentences about the reigns of the monarchs below. Mention at least one element of historical importance during each monarch's reign.**
Write your answer in about 100 words.

a. Henry VIII

b. Elizabeth I

c. Victoria

....
....
....
....
....
....
....
....
....
....
....
....
....
....
....

Great English
Monarchs
and their Times

KEY TO
THE EXERCISES
AND EXIT TEST

KEY TO THE EXERCISES

PART ONE

CHAPTER 1

Page 15 Exercise 1
a. just before his eighteenth birthday
b. his brother's widow and King
Ferdinand's only child
c. and he loved hunting and sports
d. an excellent musician
e. the Renaissance developed in
England
f. because young Henry was busy
with banquets, hunting and sports
g. his two-month old son died

Page 16 Exercise 2
became – become
was – been
died – died
married – married
loved – loved
looked – looked
had – had
spoke – spoken
studied – studied
played – played
developed – developed
began – begun

Page 17 Exercise 4
1. The symbol is a 'K' on the King's
horse.
2. a. **3.** b. **4.** a **5.** a **6.** b. **7.** b

CHAPTER 2

Page 25 Exercise 1
a. France
b. killed, English
c. ambitious, Lord Chancellor
d. religious, taxes
e. Reformation, Catholic Church
f. Piccardy, peace, France, meeting
g. money, luxury
h. Catherine, son

Page 26 Exercise 2
Dear Erasmus,
Lord Chancellor Wolsey organised an
important meeting in Piccardy
between me and the King of France.
My court and I left England on
Wednesday. We had a good sea
voyage. When we arrived it was a
sunny day. I wore my precious cloak.
Everyone was amazed.
I brought a lot of splendid clothes and
jewels.
On Friday I went hunting in the
forest.
On Saturday there was a joust.
I won of course!
It was great fun.
On Sunday the King invited me and
my court to a magnificent banquet.
We ate for seven hours!
Then we went to sleep.

Your friend, Henry

'READING' A PAINTING

Page 28 Exercise 1
1. different shades of brown, beige, cream, dark green, gold
2. c
3. b, c, d
4. a, b, c
5. c
6. c

CHAPTER 3

Page 35 Exercise 1
a. F – In 1526 Henry fell in love with Anne Boleyn and decided to divorce from his wife. But he needed permission from the Pope in Rome.
b. T
c. F – Sir Thomas More became the new Lord Chancellor of England, and Thomas Cranmer became the new Archbishop of Canterbury.
d. T
e. F – Princess Elizabeth was born in 1533 and Henry was desolate.
f. T
g. F – In May 1536 Anne Boleyn was beheaded and Henry married Jane Seymour.
h. T
i. F – Prince Edward received an excellent education from the best scholars.

Page 36 Exercise 2
Wolsey: rich, greedy, ambitious, organised a meeting in France, built Hampton Court
More: great scholar, honest man, opposed Henry's break with Rome, Lord Chancellor, was beheaded
Henry VIII: patron of the arts, rich, great scholar, wore magnificent clothes, built palaces and castles, lived in luxury

Page 37 Exercise 3
a. R
b. DS
c. W
d. R
e. W
f. R
g. DS

CHAPTER 4

Page 43 Exercise 1
a. monasteries, Wales
b. Cromwell
c. Younger, painter
d. German, strong ally
e. fifth, Catherine Howard, lovers
f. wife, Parr
g. College
h. illnesses, walk
i. death, three children

Page 43 Exercise 2
a3 b5 c4 d1 e2

Page 44 Exercise 3

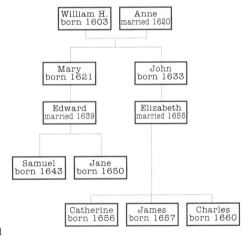

Page 45 Exercise 4

a. Catherine Howard
b. Anne Boleyn
c. Catherine Parr
d. Catherine of Aragon
e. Anne of Cleves
f. Jane Seymour

Page 46 Exercise 5

Queen	Children	Fate
Catherine of Aragon (1509-1533)	6	D
Anne Boleyn (1533-1536)	6	X
Jane Seymour (1536-1537)	B	Ø
Anne of Cleves (1540-1540)	N	D
Catherine Howard (1540-1542)	N	X
Catherine Parr (1543-1547)	N	S

PART TWO

CHAPTER 1

Page 53 Exercise 1

a. intelligent, dancing
b. daughter, Protestants
c. imprisoned, Tower
d. Elizabeth, loved
e. alert, advisers
f. William Cecil, favourites
g. progresses

Page 54 Exercise 2

a. intelligent,
b. scholar
c. virginals
d. vain
e. faith
f. Hatfield
g. loyal

Queen Elizabeth was thrifty.

Page 54 Exercise 3

a. Who
b. When
c. What
d. Why
e. Where

CHAPTER 2

Page 60 Exercise 1

a. F – Mary Stuart was a Catholic and became Queen of Scots.
b. T
c. F – Elizabeth was dangerously ill with smallpox but a German doctor saved her life.
d. T
e. F – The Scots suspected that Mary and the Earl of Bothwell killed Lord Darnley.
f. F – Mary escaped to England and became a danger for Elizabeth.
g. T
h. T

Page 60 Exercise 2

luxurious, beauty, angry, furious, danger

a. happy, luxurious
b. beautiful
c. furious
d. dangerous
e. angry

Page 61 Exercise 3

Six noble gentlemen will execute you.

CHAPTER 3

Page 69 Exercise 1

a. its empire extended to the West Indies, Central and South America
b. took gold, jewels and other riches from the natives
c. Drake, Hawkins and Cavendish
d. attack Spanish galleons and take their treasures
e. claimed California for Queen Elizabeth

f. treasure, new foods and spices

g. set up the Virginia colony in North America

Page 70 Exercise 2
a4 b6 c5 d2 e1 f3
a2 b4 c1 d3

Page 71 Exercise 3
control, problem, new, across, route, pay, best, ships, dangerous, maps, afraid, World, leave, year, sail, attack, their, find, foods, everything, honour

CHAPTER 4

Page 79 Exercise 1
a. King Philip of Spain
b. King Philip of Spain
c. 130 ships and about 28,000 men
d. eight fireships
e. it was defeated
f. William Shakespeare
g. open-air theatres in London

Page 80 Exercise 2
a2 b1 c4 d6 e7 f8 g3 h5 i9

'READING' A PAINTING

Page 84 Exercise 1
1. a. the one to the left
b. the one to the right
2. b
3. c
4. b
5. No, Yes
6. b
7. c
8. a

PART THREE

CHAPTER 1

Page 91 Exercise 1
a. lonely, mother, governess
b. 13, parts, wrote, diary
c. became, years
d. understand, government
e. they, married
f. because, foreigner
g. intelligent, him, dedicated

Page 93 Exercise 4
morning, visited, big, was, surprised, saw, houses, streets, family, lived, one, were, poor, sad, went, factory, many, worked, did, work, did, feet, was, was, school, day

CHAPTER 2

Page 100 Exercise 1
a. F – Victoria and Albert had nine children and they spent a lot of time with them.
b. T
c. F – The Penny Black was the name of the first adhesive postage stamp.
d. T
e. T
f. T
g. F – The Ten Hour Act of 1847 limited the working day of women and children to ten hours.
h. T
i. T

Page 101 Exercise 2

Crossword:

1. SMOKE
2. CHRISTMAS TREE
3. TRAIN
4. OSBORNE
5. DICKENS
6. GERMAN
7. SUBURBS
8. VICTORIA
9. MORE
10. RED
11. BIG
12. GLASS

Page 102 Exercise 4
a4 b3 c2 d5 e1

CHAPTER 3

Page 107 Exercise 1
a. helped Turkey to fight Russia
b. opened the first school for nurses
c. a special medal for courage at war
d. India became part of the British Empire
e. caught typhoid fever and died in December
f. became a recluse
g. to abolish the monarchy and create a republic

Page 108 Exercise 2
a. Prince Albert
b. Prince of Wales
c. Queen Victoria
d. Florence Nightingale
e. courageous soldiers
f. John Brown
g. some politicians
h. Queen Victoria
i. Prince Albert
j. Florence Nightingale

Page 108 Exercise 3
painful, tragic, unhappy, suffered, devastated, agony, misery, sadness
a. tragic/painful
b. suffered
c. devastated

CHAPTER 4

Page 115 Exercise 1
a. 'tube', railway
b. social reforms
c. telephone, automobile
d. Disraeli, expand
e. Suez Canal, India
f. Empress
g. missionary, Africa
h. coffee, diamonds
i. Golden Jubilee
j. biggest, land

Page 116 Exercise 2
Politicians: Disraeli, Gladstone
Explorers: Livingstone, Stanley
Inventors: Bell, (Karl Benz)
Musicians: Gilbert and Sullivan, Edward Elgar

Africa
telephone, automobile
The Mikado – HMS Pinafore – The Pirates of Penzance – the music for the Golden Jubilee celebrations
photography

1. **a.** Renaissance
   b. wives ... heir
   c. English Church
   d. monasteries ... treasures
   e. daughter ... queen ... intelligent ... moderate
   f. rival ... beheaded
   g. Sir Francis Drake ... colony
   h. defeated
   i. Shakespeare ... writer

2. **a.** T
   b. F – Henry VIII had six wives.
   c. T
   d. F – He had one son by Jane Seymour.
   e. F – She was a strong ruler.
   f. T
   g. F – He set up the Virginia colony in North America.
   h. F – Elizabeth I's reign lasted 44 years.
   i. F – Victoria became queen when she was only eighteen years old and knew very little about government or politics.
   j. T
   k. F – The Victorian Age was a period of great change.
   l. T
   m. F – The Suez Canal opened an important trade route to the East.

3. dangerous / courageous / successful / happy / beautiful / angry / luxurious / furious / healthy

4. **1.** C **2.** A **3.** D **4.** C **5.** D
   6. B **7.** D **8.** B **9.** C **10.** D
   11. D **12.** A

5. **A.** **1.** 1509
   2. Yes
   3. Three
   4. 1547
   B. **1.** 1559
   2. No
   3. None
   4. 1603
   C. **1.** 1837
   2. Yes
   3. Nine
   4. 1901

6. Open answer.

PLACES YOU CAN VISIT

尋 找 英 國 名 君 之 旅

Here are some places you can visit that are associated
with the life and times of the three monarchs in this book.

HENRY VIII

Deal Castle, Kent: The castle was built in the shape of the Tudor Rose.
Hampton Court Palace, Surrey: It was originally built as a home
for Cardinal Wolsey. It later came into the possession of Henry VIII.
Today many visitors go to Hampton Court,
which is famous for its fascinating maze.
Hever Castle, Kent: The home of the Boleyn family
where Henry VIII courted Anne.
Leeds Castle, Kent: It was originally built as a Norman fortress
and was converted into a Royal Palace by Henry VIII. It is considered
one of the loveliest and most romantic castles in the world!

ELIZABETH I

Hatfield House, Hertfordshire: Young Elizabeth spent
a lot of her time here. Many of her personal belongings are on display.
Tower of London: The Crown Jewels and other interesting collections
are found here. Numerous events in Elizabeth's life took place here.
Stratford-upon-Avon, Warwickshire: Shakespeare's birthplace
and home of the Royal Shakespeare Company.

VICTORIA

Kensington Palace, London: Victoria's birthplace,
where she spent many years of her youth.
Osborne House, Isle of Wight: One of Victoria's favourite homes.
The private apartments are exactly as Victoria left them
when she died in 1901.
Victoria and Albert Museum, London: One of the great museums
planned by Prince Albert.

Black Cat English Readers

Level 1
Peter Pan
Zorro!
American Folk Tales
The True Story of Pocahontas
Davy Crockett

Level 2
Oliver Twist
King Arthur and his Knights
Oscar Wilde's Short Stories
Robin Hood
British and American
  Festivities

Level 3
Great English Monarchs and
  their Times
Alice's Adventures in
  Wonderland
The Jumping Frog
Hamlet
The Secret Garden

Level 4
The £1,000,000 Bank Note
Jane Eyre
Sherlock Holmes Investigates
Gulliver's Travels
The Strange Case of Dr Jekyll
  and Mr Hyde
Classic Detective Stories
The Phantom of the Opera
Alien at School
Romeo and Juliet
Treasure Island

Level 5
A Christmas Carol
The Tragedy of Dr Faustus
Washington Square
A Midsummer Night's Dream
American Horror
Much Ado About Nothing
The Canterbury Tales
Dracula
The Last of the Mohicans
The Big Mistake and Other
  Stories

Level 6
Frankenstein
Pride and Prejudice
Robinson Crusoe
A Tale of Two Cities
The X-Files : Squeeze

BLACK CAT ENGLISH CLUB

Membership Application Form

BLACK CAT ENGLISH CLUB is for those who love English reading and seek for better English to share and learn with fun together.

Benefits offered:
- *Membership Card*
- *Member badge, poster, bookmark*
- *Book discount coupon*
- *Black Cat English Reward Scheme*
- *English learning e-forum*
- *Surprise gift and more...*

Simply fill out the application form below and fax it back to 2565 1113.

Join Now! It's FREE exclusively for readers who have purchased *Black Cat English Readers* !

The book(or book set) that you have purchased: _____

English Name: _____ (Surname) _____ (Given Name)

Chinese Name: _____

Address: _____

Tel: _____ Fax: _____

Email: _____
(Login password for e-forum will be sent to this email address.)

Sex: ❏ Male ❏ Female

Education Background: ❏ Primary 1-3 ❏ Primary 4-6 ❏ Junior Secondary Education (F1-3)
❏ Senior Secondary Education (F4-5) ❏ Matriculation
❏ College ❏ University or above

Age: ❏ 6 - 9 ❏ 10 - 12 ❏ 13 - 15 ❏ 16 - 18 ❏ 19 - 24 ❏ 25 - 34
❏ 35 - 44 ❏ 45 - 54 ❏ 55 or above

Occupation: ❏ Student ❏ Teacher ❏ White Collar ❏ Blue Collar
❏ Professional ❏ Manager ❏ Business Owner ❏ Housewife
❏ Others (please specify: _____)

As a member, what would you like **BLACK CAT ENGLISH CLUB** to offer:
❏ Member gathering/ party ❏ English class with native teacher ❏ English competition
❏ Newsletter ❏ Online sharing ❏ Book fair
❏ Book discount ❏ Others (please specify: _____)

Other suggestions to **BLACK CAT ENGLISH CLUB**:

_____

Please sign here: _____

(Date: _____)